HOT JOCKS 1

PLAYING
FOR KEEPS

New York Times & *USA Today* Bestselling Author

KENDALL RYAN

Playing for Keeps
Copyright © 2019 Kendall Ryan

Content Editing by
Elaine York, and Rachel Brookes

Copy Editing by
Rose Hilliard

Proofreading by
Virginia Tesi-Carey

Cover Design and Formatting by
Uplifting Designs & Marketing

ABOUT THE BOOK

I've never been so stupid in my entire life.

My teammate's incredibly sweet and gorgeous younger sister should have been off-limits, but my hockey stick didn't get that memo.

After our team won the championship, and plenty of alcohol, our flirting turned physical and I took her to bed.

Shame sent her running the next morning from our catastrophic mistake. She thinks I don't remember that night—but every detail is burned into my brain so deeply, I'll never forget. The feel of her in my arms, the soft whimpers of pleasure I coaxed from her perfect lips...

And now I've spent three months trying to get her out of my head. Which has been futile, because I'm starting to understand she's the only girl I'll ever want.

I have one shot to show her I can be exactly what she needs, but Elise won't be easily convinced.

That's okay, because I'm good under pressure, and this time, I'm playing for keeps.

Get ready to meet your new favorite hot jocks in this series of stand-alone novels. If you like sexy, confident men who know how to handle a stick (on and off the ice), and smart women who are strong enough to keep all those big egos in check, this series of athlete romances is perfect for you!

PLAYLIST

"No Tears Left to Cry" by Ariana Grande

"Sit Next to Me" by Foster the People

"Pardon Me" by Incubus

"First" by Cold War Kids

"Midnight City" by M83

"I Miss You" by Blink 182

"Can't Hold Us" by Macklemore and Ryan Lewis

"Sail" by Awolnation

CHAPTER ONE

Unruly Hockey Players

Justin

I have a beautiful woman sitting in my lap.

I don't know her name, or what she does for a living, or where she grew up.

I do know that she smells like tequila... and that tequila and I have never played particularly well together.

But none of that matters to her.

The only thing that matters is that I'm a pro hockey athlete, and so she's ready to fuck me. Which holds exactly zero appeal for me.

Don't get me wrong, I love female attention, but lately every minute of it all feels stale, like I've been there, seen that, done it all before and have the t-shirt to prove it.

I'm not even sure she knows my name. But I'd bet good money on her knowing my jersey number by heart. I guess that's why they call the women jersey chasers, or in hockey—puck bunnies.

"Justin Motherfuckin' Brady!" Owen, my best friend and roommate, calls from our living room. "Get a drink and get your balls in here."

I nod and flash him a thumbs-up.

"You'll have to excuse me," I say to the petite brunette currently running her hands down my chest.

She blinks at me with lust-filled blue eyes. After a moment's hesitation, she hops up from my lap with a frown and I slide off of the barstool.

"If you want to score tonight, I'm a sure thing, cutie," she says with a flirty wink.

I rub one hand over my jaw. This shit is really getting old. "I'm good. Thanks, though."

I'm sure I sound like an asshole, but whatever. I can feel her eyes on me as I walk away.

The party was already in full swing by the time I made it home a little while ago. The marble countertops are littered with empty beer bottles, most of them imported or pricey craft brews. A few bottles of flavored vodka along with fruity mixers are on the island—Owen's attempt at being welcoming to the scantily-clad ladies scattered around the apartment—most of whom are perched in players' laps and draped over the sectional in the living room.

I probably sound like an old man at the ripe age of twenty-eight, but this is hardly fun anymore. Some nights I just want to go to bed...alone and in blissful peace and quiet. Yep, it's official, I need to apply for my AARP discounts and hand over my man card...stat.

Grabbing a six-pack of beer from the counter, I head into the living room. The guys are in rare form tonight. Winning the league championship will do that, I guess.

"Is that really Justin Brady?" a redhead asks from behind me as I head through the kitchen. I'm sure I look different without twenty pounds of hockey gear on, but the cynical side of me thinks about how inter-changeable the players are for girls like her. Bragging rights that you've bagged a pro player is practically the name of the game. Not that being someone's conquest has ever really bothered me before. But something about it annoys me as I weave my way through bodies.

Our star center, Asher, reaches out to bump his fist against mine as I walk past. "Awesome play tonight."

"Thanks, dude."

Someone hands me a shot as I pass and I down it without bothering to look what's in the glass.

Most of the team isn't just celebrating our win tonight. They're celebrating the fact that the off-season has just begun and a summer break of zero responsibilities is right around the corner.

Me? Not so much.

I eat, drink, and breathe hockey and so the idea of six weeks without the rigorous schedule to distract me is my own personal brand of hell.

I didn't have the easiest time growing up, and the breakdown of my family only made me play faster, fight harder, take more chances—and that's why we're winners celebrating tonight.

That said, when the two people who are supposed to love you unconditionally use you as nothing more than a pawn in their sick games, it warps your view on love. I wasn't lovable—I knew that. I'd known that since I was six years old. And nothing had changed in the last twenty years. Women wanted me for my dick, and that was fine. That was really all I had to offer anyway.

I take up one half of the sofa, and work on polishing off my beer.

Teddy King, one of our best forwards and a total player, is making out with a girl in the corner.

"TK, get a fuckin' room!" someone calls out.

It's no surprise that Owen is on the couch with two blondes in his lap. He's my best friend, but the dude is a notorious player. "I hope you ladies are good at sharing," Owen says over the thumping music.

The blondes smile at each other, one of them turning to blink up at him. "And what will we be sharing?"

"My dick," he says, matter-of-factly.

The girls begin to giggle like he's just said the most interesting thing in the world.

I roll my eyes and open another beer from the six-pack at my feet.

Owen is six foot four and well over two hundred pounds of muscle with messy brown hair and the stubble of a beard he hasn't bothered to shave since we made the playoffs. He's one of the best goalies in the entire league, and he knows he's the shit. He's cocky, but he's earned the right to be. He plays it up well, and is known to be a total ladies' man. And the girls eat that shit up.

Normally I'd be doing the same exact thing, looking to blow off steam and celebrate our win, but tonight I can't seem to get out of my head long enough to relax. I'm more than a hard dick. I'm more than what I can do with a hockey stick. But most of these people here don't know that. Hell, I'm not even sure I know that anymore.

The only person here who looks to be as uneasy as me is Owen's younger sister, Elise. She's standing across the room, arms folded over her chest with her lips pressed into a firm line. The three of us grew up together a few hours from here in central Washington. I've known her since she was a bossy first-grader with a gap between her front teeth, and always wearing those shiny patent-leather shoes with frilly dresses.

Her looks, and her sense of fashion, have changed quite a bit. Her attitude, not so much. I can tell she's pissed about how out of hand things have gotten. I'm sure she'll be the first one here in the morning, nursing hangovers and helping us clean the apartment. There are at least fifty people here, and I know less than half of them.

A few seconds later, like she's heard my inner thoughts, Elise wanders closer and sits down next to me on the sofa. She looks so damn small in an oversized jersey and a pair of leggings. It's strange because most girls here are dressed in tiny black dresses that barely cover their asses and too much makeup, but Elise is nothing like that. Sometimes I forget she's all grown up, that she graduated from college last year, and is an actual adult.

"Hey, E." I raise my beer toward hers.

"Hey. Congrats on tonight."

"Thanks," I mutter after another long swig of beer. "You're not drinking?" I ask.

"I've had a couple," she says, her gaze still scanning the party, almost like she's making a concentrated effort not to look at me.

I know the feeling.

Normally—I see something I want—and I go and get it. It's how I've always been. It's how I'm wired. The one exception to that rule? Elise Parrish.

She's a no-fly zone. She used to be the cute kid sister of my best friend, but something shifted recently and I went from thinking of her as Owen's younger sister to something more.

This was the girl who borrowed my sweatshirts and never returned them. Took my warmest gloves and lost one somewhere between home and the ice rink. The girl who followed me and Owen around like a lost puppy all throughout our childhoods and the girl who cried during sappy commercials.

I had no idea how badly I would miss all those things about her until I moved away for college. But then my life got so busy with school and exams and hockey and fighting for a spot in the pros, my fascination with Elise took a backseat, and I knew it was for the best.

Still, despite my best efforts, she traipsed out of friend territory somewhere along the way, and into a sexy woman who made my dick ache. It was dangerous. And my best friend Owen made no apologies for the fact that his sister was very much off-limits to any member of our team.

My gaze drifts over to her again, and my breath catches. She's beautiful, intoxicatingly so. But she's smart too. And feisty. And she knows the game of hockey better than most of the guys, Lord knows she grew up spending just as much time at the ice rink as we did. Plus, the fact that I'm a pro hockey player doesn't impress her in the slightest. That's the best thing about her. I can just be myself.

"How pissed off are you?" I ask, unable to hide the amusement in my voice.

Elise shakes her head, the smirk on her mouth unmistakable. "On a scale of one to I'm going to murder Owen?"

"Sure." I polish off the rest of my beer and wait for her to answer, but she doesn't say anything else, she just lets out an exasperated sigh. So I grab another from the six-pack resting on the polished wood floor beneath my feet. "Want one?" I offer her a beer, but she shakes her head.

I drain half the bottle watching Asher and Teddy flirt with a group of girls on the balcony. They're eyeing the hot tub, which I'm suddenly sure will have floating remnants of jizz in the morning. Fucking fantastic.

"Those fuckers better not take those bunnies in the hot tub," Elise says under her breath.

I swallow a chuckle and shake my head. "You're good peeps, E," I mumble, feeling the effects of the alcohol already.

Elise shakes her head, a smile tugging up her full lips. "I'm the freaking best. Someone's got to babysit this idiot team."

I study her for just a second. Long dark hair hanging over one shoulder, grey eyes that always seem to see straight through me, along with a sassy mouth that has always called me out on my bullshit.

But I never let myself notice things like that about her, and I won't start now, so I look down at the beer bottle in my hands instead.

When she's beside me, all my nerve endings light up with a feeling I can't explain.

I feel alive.

Raw.

On edge.

And there's no point in denying it–a whole lot turned on.

I need to get myself in check, but instead I'm feeling a little reckless. Unsteady.

"You know what will make this situation better?" I ask, sneaking one more glance at her.

"What's that?"

"Vodka."

Elise shakes her head.

"Come on, E-Class."

This earns me a laugh. The old nickname I bestowed on her in eighth grade still strikes a chord.

"I'll slice the lemons, you get the glasses?" she asks.

My heart starts to beat faster as she grins up at me. *Well damn, I didn't know I still had one of those.*

I smile back. "It's on."

CHAPTER TWO

The Vodka Was a Terrible Idea

Elise

It's way past my bedtime. So why haven't I gone home yet?

Oh right, because I'm babysitting my idiot brother and his teammates. As per usual.

And considering that they won a national championship tonight—they're in an especially celebratory mood. We started off at the sports bar near the rink, but when things got too crazy being out in public with some overzealous fans, we moved the party back to my brother Owen and his BFF Justin's penthouse.

Owen, my disgusting slut of a brother, is feeling up one blonde on the couch while his tongue is down another's throat. The sad thing? I'll probably be responsible for kicking both of these naked ass girls out of his bed tomorrow morning.

Awesome.

TK and Asher are in the hot tub with no fewer than five girls between them. No, scratch that, there's six of them—one chick's head just surfaced from under the water. Just freaking wonderful.

I'm never going in that hot tub again.

Justin hasn't hooked up with anyone yet, and I'm just waiting for it to happen. He's been all strangely sad and mopey tonight and I'm not sure what the hell is going on with him.

But I do know one thing—the shots I took with him were a bad idea. One shot, shame on us, multiple shots, shame on me. I know my limit, and doing shots with Justin is a hard line I shouldn't have crossed.

I know I should see him as nothing more than a disgusting manwhore, or see him as a second brother to me—but I've never felt anything remotely familial about Justin Brady like I should. First there's my traitorous body—which reacts to his in a very non-sisterly way. So much so, my lady parts are tingling and I'm pretty sure there's a tiny damp spot in my panties from when he smiled and pushed my hair behind my shoulder as he watched me drain my shot glass for the umpteenth time and suck on the lemon slice afterwards.

Then there's my heart, which pumps faster whenever he's near and does stupid shit like ache for him when he takes a hard hit on the ice. It's all like please don't have broken anything adorable or important.

But finally, there's my head—which knows without a doubt that this man is bad for me. My head wins out, which meant I finally extracted myself from beside him on the sofa, leaving him to polish off most of the bottle of vodka alone. Everyone else is drinking like they're celebrating. Justin is drinking like he's trying to numb some indescribable pain that I know isn't hockey related.

I've always been enamored with him, from his quiet confidence, to his dedication and hard work on the ice, to his hard won smiles and casual attitude.

The physical changes he went through as we aged made me fall even harder. Instead of being the boy who pulled my ponytail and hid my dolls from me, he grew from a lanky teen into a man. A man with so much sculpted muscle and iron-carved abs it made my knees weak.

It's late—or early, depending on how you look at it, and about half of the guests have left. The team and their bunnies are still here, but I'm guessing people will begin coupling off and disappearing into bedrooms soon. I clean up the kitchen a little bit, throwing empty bottles away and bagging up the garbage that's been left out on the counters.

Owen has disappeared with the two blondes, and the door to the media room is now closed, which is where he's probably taken them since he has a weird rule about not bringing hookups to his bed. Public displays of drunken sex are never a good thing, especially when one of those people is your brother, so I'm just grateful they're behind a closed door, although I know I'll be forced to see some of their prime real estate when I kick their hungover selves out in a few hours. God help me. Teddy and Asher are still in the hot tub with the group of women, and Justin is still on the couch where I left him, drinking party of one.

I've had more to drink than I should have, and decide that it's probably time to say goodnight and get myself home. After I toss a few more empties in the trash, I lean one hip against the counter and fish my cell out of my back pocket to request a ride to come pick me up. I just need to use the restroom first.

The guest bathroom in the hallway is occupied, and after I wait for a few minutes, and no one emerges, I knock again. Then I hear moaning coming from inside.

Gross. Is it too much to ask any person here to have some shame?

Plan B.

I head to Justin's bedroom at the end of the hall to use the en-suite attached to his room. I have to pee and I know I won't make it the twenty-minute ride home. Plus, I know Justin won't mind.

When I enter, I can't help but inhale deeply. His room smells like him. His scent hasn't changed in all the years I've known him. The smell is a combination of an understanding boyfriend, clean cotton, and a bar of soap. It's fucking amazing, and I'm in his personal space alone, so I inhale more of it than I should. What can I say? I'm greedy like that.

The space is neat and organized, his king-sized bed dressed in fluffy white linens and a handful of personal items are lined up neatly on the dresser. A phone charger. His wallet. A leather watch. A bottle of cologne. A small day planner. His tablet.

My mind immediately wonders if he watches porn on that tablet while in bed. I have no idea what's wrong with me, but that downright sinful thought pops into my brain and refuses to evacuate. *Geez, Elise. Get it together.*

A bulky, masculine leather chair sits in the corner, and the floor lamp beside it glows softly, lighting my way to the bathroom door at the far end of the room. When I reach the bathroom, I flip on the light switch, and then turn off the lamp. Wasting electricity is a strange pet peeve of mine, and burning lamps in an unoccupied room are at the top of that list.

I enter and do my business, not daring—but so wanting—to linger over the bottles of men's products on the counter. Shaving cream. Toothpaste. A brand of deodorant I've never heard of.

A sound from behind the door catches my attention. I quickly wash my hands and exit, hoping I haven't interrupted Justin bringing a girl to his bed. Talk about a dagger through the fucking heart.

When I open the door, instead of finding him with a woman like I expect, he's alone. He's sitting on the edge of the mattress with his head in his hands. I'm not sure what I've interrupted, but it's clear he wants to be alone. Which means I need to make my presence known and exit stage right like as soon as humanly possible.

"I'm sorry. I just needed to use the bathroom. I'll go," I say, crossing the room in my quest for the exit.

But as I try to pass, one strong hand reaches out for me, gripping my legging-covered thigh. I stop in front of him, my breath caught in my throat.

"Stay," he says, still not looking up at me.

I wait for him to make a joking remark, maybe call me by one of the old nicknames he hasn't used in a while. E-Class. Easy E. But he doesn't.

"What is it? What's wrong?" My heart pounds out an uneven rhythm as I wait for him to respond.

And then he does…just not with words.

His hand slides up my thigh, and stops when it meets my hip. His grip on my hip holds me in place, but he doesn't move any further. My entire body is tingling—because this is *Justin*, my brother's best friend and roommate, and despite my many dreams and fantasies about this exact moment, he has never, not once, touched me like this. All I can think about, besides where his hands will travel to next, is the fact that he's as buzzed as I am, if not more, and liquid courage is never a good gauge for true feelings, only bad decisions.

My lungs burn with exertion. I feel like I've just run a mile and I have no idea why.

I take a deep breath, but before I can say anything else, he's rising to his feet, and standing at his full height, towering over me at six foot two inches and two hundred plus pounds of pure muscle. His shoulders are so broad that I feel tiny by comparison, and even more unsure about what I'm doing here.

But then his hands move to my face, cupping my jawline with his big, calloused palms and I forget how to breathe all over again.

"Stay," he whispers again.

Suddenly I wish I'd left on the lamp, wish I could see the expression on his face right now. His voice sounds more anguished than I've ever heard, and there's barely enough moonlight to make out his eyes.

His thumbs move over my skin, skittering along slowly as he sweeps one over the swell of my bottom lip.

"What is it?" I whisper.

Justin shakes his head, eyes closed. He drops his head until his forehead is pressed against mine.

I'm not sure I've ever seen him this vulnerable. This exposed. He's normally all masculine energy, so relaxed and in control of every situation. Tonight I feel like he could fall apart at any moment and it's unnerving me and causing my nurturing tendencies to go into overdrive.

"Tell me what you need," I whisper, placing my hands on his waist. He feels so solid beneath my palms.

"You," he croaks out, voice raw. "On the bed."

I don't even consider denying his request, which makes zero sense because we've most certainly never had an encounter like this before. I sit down on the side of his bed, and Justin sinks down next to me. But rather than let me stay where I've parked myself, on the edge of the mattress, he lifts me and moves me to the center and toward the headboard where he stretches out beside me, lying on his side.

He's big and muscular, and it feels so surreal to be here next to him. I've never even let myself imagine how this moment might feel, despite all my many fantasies about this exact moment. His brown hair is messy and his deep blue eyes are currently closed. But God, he's gorgeous with his bulky shoulders and arms, a chest that was made for nestling close against, and eight perfectly carved abs.

"You're so soft," he says, voice filled with wonder as his palm works under my shirt and lands on my stomach.

My lungs stop working as his palm slides upward, over my breastbone until his fingertips touch my throat. Then his hand moves back down, down past my belly button until he stops over my pubic bone. My pussy feels so hot and tender, and *oh-my-God*, I want his hand to move lower so badly. But he doesn't move any lower. His hand rests on my belly and I turn my face toward his.

"Justin?" His name leaves my lips only a second before his mouth presses against mine.

His kiss is so soft at first, then his fingers thread into the hair at the back of my neck as he turns my face toward his and deepens our connection.

My lips part for his, and Justin takes full advantage, sliding his tongue against mine. His kisses are everything I imagined they would be—hungry, hot, hard. A flicker of lust curls inside me.

His mouth moves over mine and when my tongue eagerly tangles with his, a low rumbling sound vibrates in his chest. All of my muscles clench at once. He tastes like lemons, and vodka, and every sinful pleasure imaginable, and dear God, I don't ever want to stop kissing him.

CHAPTER THREE

The Morning After

Elise

My entire body feels like I've been in a car accident—from my pounding head to the unexplainably sore muscles below my waist. My mouth is bone dry, and as I blink open my eyes, I have to focus on my breathing to calm the queasiness in my stomach.

Whose bed did I fall asleep in?

I shift to my side and it takes me several long seconds to realize where the hell I am.

Panic hits me the moment my eyes focus.

I look over my shoulder and see that a very naked Justin Brady is still asleep beside me.

His broad back with its lightly tanned skin

slopes down to the most mouth-watering naked ass I've ever seen on a man. Firm. Muscled. Delectable.

A thousand vivid mental images crash into my brain at once. My hands on that firm, rounded ass as he thrust into me. Those trim hips snapping between my parted thighs.

I whimper, and scramble over the side of the bed in a hunt for my clothes. And my sanity, because what the hell did I do last night? What did *we* do last night?

I remember coming in here to use the bathroom. Remember finding Justin sitting on his bed, looking somber. Then I remember kissing him. Oh my God, the kissing. I feel weak at the memory of his hot, wet tongue sliding against mine.

I find my underwear first, and pull those on— inside out, but who cares about that right now. I toss on my bra and jersey next. The jersey with my brother's number on the back. *Oh my God, Owen.* He's going to kill me if he sees me leaving Justin's room. Actually, he'll kill Justin first. And it will be bloody. I can't witness Justin's murder this morning. Because I will definitely vomit on the floor if that happens.

My leggings are nowhere to be found. I can't exactly sneak out of here pantless. *Fuck me. What had I been thinking?* I'd always lusted after Justin, but secretly lusting after him and sleeping with him are two very, *very* different things.

Yet I distinctly remember being the one to push things further. We'd been kissing on his bed, and I'd been the one to take off my shirt and then his hands traveled along my waist, my ribs, my shoulders. His touch had been my undoing —I'd been the first one to stick my hand down his pants. It was like throwing accelerant onto the fire quietly burning between us.

How drunk had he been? Way drunker than me, I know that much. Had I taken advantage of him?

Just as I'm about to have a full-blown panic attack, I spot my leggings. They're tangled in the sheets at the end of the bed. The memory of Justin kneeling before me as he slowly peeled them off jumps into my head. I'd been so hot, so ready for him. I remember practically attacking his belt-buckle with gusto in my efforts to free his erection.

Oh my God. His dick.

Now that I've pictured it, I can't unsee it. The memory of his steely shaft and heavy balls are not details I'm supposed to be in possession of. The helpless plea he'd made when my fist curled around him for the first time, testing the weight of him against my palm... I'd dragged my hand up slowly as he released a shuddering exhale, his whole body shivering.

My heartrate triples with the memory. I squeeze my eyes shut and pull a deep, shaky breath into my lungs. *Focus, Elise.* You cannot think about his dick right now. You certainly can't think about the way it tasted, or how it felt ...

Tiptoeing to the end of the bed, I reach for my leggings, and give them a swift tug. Justin shifts at the movement, rolling up on his elbow to see who's woken him. His dark hair is messy from sleep, but his blue eyes are bright and alert. A five o'clock shadow dusts his strong jaw and his chest muscles are immaculate.

I don't think I've ever used the word immaculate to describe someone before, but trust me, it fits him.

His eyes widen as he takes in the sight of me—standing at the end of his bed, naked from the waist down—and he blinks twice. "Elise?" His voice is pure gravel, and my stomach tightens.

"Yeah?"

Realizing he's naked, Justin sits up, tugging the sheet up to cover his lap, like he's suddenly self-conscious—like he wasn't inside me a few hours ago.

Oh God.

He's still watching me but he doesn't say anything else as I free my leggings from the blankets and pull them on. Yeah, I really might vomit. *Shit, this is awful.*

He pushes one hand through his messy hair, his bicep flexing with the effort. "Last night ..." Confusion is etched across his gorgeous features as he works on remembering what happened, and I swear to God, if he doesn't say something in the next three seconds, I'm going to cry.

Tears threaten behind my eyes and I take another slow, shaky breath.

Some part of me needs him to acknowledge this mountain between us. Needs him to laugh and make some joke that we've really *cemented our friendship now*— or any lighthearted remark that will make last night mean something more than just being a colossal mistake, a huge dark mark on our friendship. I need him to say something that will make it all better. *Anything but silence.*

But he stays quiet, as if he's trying to piece together what happened between us. The silence stretches on and on, and I start to grow uneasy. If he doesn't remember last night, I'm going to die of humiliation. *Was I that unmemorable?*

"Nothing happened," I blurt, unable to take his stony silence any longer.

"Right. Nothing happened," he echoes. He looks more convinced than I feel.

My heart squeezes painfully in my chest. *Does he really not remember?*

His phone chirps from the bedside table, but Justin makes no move to grab it. He's still watching me. He's still *naked.* And he doesn't look nearly as worried as I feel. Does he seriously not remember last night? Any of it? The soft grunts he made into my neck as he thrust above me will be forever burned into my brain. The feel of his body moving over mine is a memory I'll never be able to erase. The ache in my thighs and the tingle of my lady parts will fade, but I have a feeling my tattered heart will take much longer to recover.

"Don't panic, okay?"

"I'm not!" I snap, a little too quickly. He must have read the panic in my eyes, in my stiff posture, but I can't help it. I am panicking. Big freaking time.

His phone chirps again, filling the awkward silence between us. An empty condom wrapper rests next to his phone and oh my God my cheeks are as red as a tomato. I can feel it.

"You should probably grab that. I'm going to go," I stammer.

Some unreadable emotion flashes across his features, but he reaches for the phone and I scamper toward the door, needing to get away from this fucked up situation as fast as possible.

CHAPTER FOUR

Secrets

Elise

The apartment is quiet as I move through the living room and kitchen. Thank God Owen's not up yet. I'd much prefer to do this walk of shame in private. In fact, I don't know how I'll ever meet my brother's eyes ever again. Last night was completely out of character for me.

I find my phone and my purse where I left them and turn toward the door when I see movement from down the hall that stops me dead in my guilt-ridden tracks.

It's my brother. Dressed only in a pair of athletic shorts, his hair is sticking up in six different directions.

"Hey," Owen says, eyeing me curiously. His

voice is gravelly from sleep, and he stretches his arms over his head. "You stay here last night?"

"No!" I say quickly before composing myself. I have to swallow the bile in my throat before continuing with my lie. "I just came by to see if you guys wanted coffee. Figured you'd be hungover."

"You're the fuckin' best," Owen groans. He either doesn't notice, or doesn't call me out on the fact I'm still wearing last night's clothes. "I need coffee. Like eight Tylenol. And maybe a breakfast sandwich from Tito's?" he asks, mouth curving into a hopeful grin.

I roll my eyes and let out a sigh. It's a little breakfast place we all love, but it's always packed on a Sunday. "Fine. But if I have to wait in line for Tito's, you have to come to my classroom on Career Day and tell my students about your job."

"Deal," he agrees.

"And you're paying."

Owen grabs his wallet from his bedroom and emerges with his black card, which he hands me no questions asked. "Thanks, sis."

"And I don't want to run in to any of last night's conquests. Get rid of them before I get back." I narrow my eyes at him and shove the card in my purse.

"Done." Owen never lets his bunnies sleep over, but there are bound to be a few of them lingering. His gaze cuts over toward Justin's bedroom door, which is still closed. "I think Brady had an overnight guest too. I heard them going at it. But yeah, I'll clear everyone out by the time you get back."

My heart hammers wildly in my chest. My own brother heard me fucking his friend last night. And Justin doesn't even remember it. Welcome to the worst best day of my life. It doesn't get much worse than this, folks.

When I make it back to the apartment thirty minutes later, Owen and Justin have made a significant dent in the cleanup efforts.

I pass out the coffees and breakfast sandwiches to the guys—Teddy and Asher are still here too, and everyone is nursing an obvious hangover. Luckily, Owen stuck to his end of the bargain because any overnight guests are gone.

I sip my coffee and listen to my brother and Asher trade stories about their conquests from last night.

"You disappeared early last night, Brady,"

Owen says to Justin, a smirk on his lips. "Who was the hottie in your bed last night?"

I wait for Justin's eyes to stray over to mine, but thankfully they don't.

"No one," Justin says in a voice so convincing I can't help but believe he means it.

I keep it together just long enough not to arouse any suspicions, and then I leave, ducking out into the hall where the tears start falling before I even reach the elevator.

Fleeing the scene of the crime is a necessity, but going home alone is the last thing on my mind. I text my bestie, Becca, while in route to her place.

`I need alcohol.`

She replies when I'm sitting in the back of the Uber. She doesn't bother pointing out it's only ten in the morning.

`What happened?`

`Justin Fucking Brady.`

She knows how I feel about him. My stupid,

secret crush wasn't a secret I could ever keep from her. We have very few of those between us, if any.

Oh girl.

She follows up her last text up with the knife emoji and I chuckle alone in the back of the car like a crazy person.

A few minutes later, the driver pulls to a stop in front of her apartment, and Becca lets me inside and pulls me into a big hug.

"What the fuck did he do now?"

I knew she was probably thinking that he'd done something insensitive like hooked up with a jersey chaser right in front me. The truth is obviously much worse. And not something I'm going to blurt out on her doorstep.

Becca leads me inside and then stops in the kitchen to pour herself a mug of coffee. "Want some of this? I have vodka too if you were serious about the alcohol."

"Oh God," I groan. "I'm never drinking vodka again."

I help myself to a bottle of water from her

fridge and follow Becca into the living room.

"What the hell happened after I left?" she asks.

Becca had been at the bar with us after the game. She's close friends with my brother too, but she's not a big partier, so she'd opted to go home instead of come back to Owen and Justin's place.

I let out a heavy sigh. I might as well get this over with. Time to rip off the band aid.

"I slept with Justin last night." It feels so weird to say that out loud.

Becca's hand flies up to her mouth. "Oh my God. Like …?"

"Yeah."

"But," she starts.

"Yeah," I repeat.

"What happened? I don't understand."

That makes two of us. One second I was standing in his room, and the next I was on his bed with my hands in his hair as he kissed the daylights out of me.

"We drank together. He seemed so sad. It wasn't like him. Then we started kissing and …"

Tears form in my eyes and I blink rapidly.

"Where did this happen?" Becca asks.

"In his room."

"Owen doesn't know?"

I shake my head, curling my legs up on the couch. "No one knows. Not even Justin."

Becca's brows shoot up and she makes a face of surprise. "Umm …how is that possible?"

"This morning we woke up beside each other, and he didn't even remember last night. I don't know what he thinks happened." I take a deep breath, holding it in my lungs. I release the breath slowly, my heart aching. "He took my v-card, Becca, and he doesn't even know it."

Becca moves closer on the couch and pulls me in for another hug. "Oh, sweetie. Fuck him. What an asshole."

Silent tears spill down my cheeks as I let her hug me. She knows my entire history with Justin. Our friendship growing up. My secret longing. She's had a front row seat to it all for years now.

When I pull myself together, she hands me a box of tissues.

"It's not all his fault, Becca. I was there too. I may have even initiated it. The sex, I mean." I hang my head in shame because I most definitely did initiate it.

"Here's the thing, Elise. People treat you the way you let them."

I roll my eyes. "Sheesh, that sounds like a line out of a self-help book."

She shrugs. "If the shoe fits, babe."

Becca isn't normally the type to dish out such tough love, which tells me that I really made a colossal mistake hooking up with Justin last night. He's a friend, sure. But he's also a manwhore times a hundred and isn't exactly known for his thoughtful respect or careful consideration of the opposite sex. I guess I hoped I would be the exception to that rule. Stupid, I know.

"Well it's never happening again, so it doesn't matter."

It does matter. It matters more than anything, but I can't let Becca be right. The concerned expression on her face is more than I can take right now. I'm not only nursing a massive hangover, but a broken heart too.

"Are you okay?" she asks.

"I will be." I have to be. It's not like I have a choice. He lives with my brother. Even if I make avoiding him an Olympic sport—I'm still bound to run into the guy.

She squeezes my shoulder. Then she grins. "Well... was he at least good in the sack?"

I laugh for the first time all day. "Oh my God, Becca!"

She chuckles, smiling at me. "What? I just want to know if the rumors are true."

I know exactly which rumors she's referring to. That his dick is huge. That he's a giver in bed. That his stamina rivals that of the Energizer Bunny. They are all true. All except for one. From whispered conversations I'd overheard at various events over the years, I thought he didn't like kissing. That one was proven false since we spent a long time making out on his bed. And I can say with certainty that the man is a damn good kisser. Passionate, but not sloppy.

"I don't want to think about it," I croak out finally.

Becca nods. "It's probably better that way. You

need to move on. How can he not even remember or realize that he took your virginity? Asshole," she says firmly.

She's right. He's never going to be the man I need. This morning cemented what I'd secretly already known. "I know. You're right."

"Today, tears," she says, patting my back. "Tomorrow, we plot his murder and take over the world."

I sniff loudly and nod in agreement. I still feel gutted, but at least I have Becca to make me smile.

CHAPTER FIVE

The Smell of Regret

Justin

It's been three days since we won the championship game, and I think half the team is still hungover. Myself included.

I skate past Owen and he gives me a one-finger salute.

"This fucking blows, dude," he groans, huffing after me.

I force a smile and nod at him. He wouldn't be skating beside me, casually shooting the shit if he knew what I did to his baby sister Saturday night. My stomach tightens and I swallow down a wave of remorse, then push myself harder. My lungs burn and my thigh muscles ache with the effort, but the cut of my skates against the ice is the only thing keeping me grounded at the moment.

It's a team skate, and the official start to the off-season. Later, we'll listen to coach's expectations of us, mostly related to public conduct and social media, and then Grant, our captain, will give a talk too. Finally, we'll do locker cleanout, which will only take twenty minutes or so, and then we'll be free for a couple of weeks until the rigors of training camp start.

My agent has lined up several public appearances for me in the next couple of days, and I'm going to shoot a commercial next week. I know I should feel grateful and excited for the time off, but considering all I want to do is play hockey, I'm really not looking forward to the downtime.

Plus, more downtime means more time to think. And thinking about my night with Elise is the last thing I can let myself do.

I can barely look at Owen without feeling sick to my stomach over what I did. Waves of nausea hit me—out of fear he'll find out, or over regret over what happened, I'm not sure.

It doesn't matter that that night was the best night of my life. It doesn't matter that in the morning, I wanted to hold her, wanted to kiss her, talk with her, ask what she was thinking, how she was feeling. Because the second I opened my eyes, I saw the regret written all over her face. From head to toe, she looked so uncomfortable. I let her believe I didn't remember any of it. What else could I do? And when she'd practically bolted out of my room, I'd grabbed my phone to see a text from a girl I hooked up with a couple of months before while on the road in Tennessee saying she was pregnant. It cemented everything. I wouldn't infect Elise with my bullshit.

Even if I had been willing to come clean to Owen and risk my friendship, I knew Elise deserved someone better. Not a dirtbag like me who got some girl in another state pregnant. I fuck up everything I touch, and I won't do that to her.

I slow my pace and let a couple of the guys sail past me, trying to catch my breath, when I turn and get broadsided by Asher shoulder-checking me into the plexiglass.

"We're three days into the off-season. Already gone soft, Brady?" Asher calls over his shoulder as he skates away.

Fucker.

"Fuck you too!" I call out as he whizzes past.

"Play nice, boys," Grant says, looking between us.

The truth is, I've never done well in the off-season. Not even back in high school—though I refused to think about the reasons why that might be—like my parents' nasty divorce that stretched on for far too long.

Both of them wanting to hang onto me like I was some prize. Fighting over full custody had nothing to do with how much they loved me, and everything to do with the little hockey prodigy I was that would have the potential to earn millions one day. Which I do, in spite of all their drama.

I catch up to Asher, who's retelling the story about his shenanigans in the hot tub for the third time. Since I've heard the story multiple times already, I know which parts to laugh at, which is good because I'm so unfocused, I can't concentrate for shit. I don't think anyone on the team can tell something's bothering me, and that's exactly the way I want it. I can't have people asking what's wrong. Who knows what the fuck is liable to come out of my mouth.

But I'm so distracted by thoughts of Elise, I can barely focus.

The memory of her in my bed, kneeling in front of me as she reached one hand out and rubbed my hard length through my jeans. Her lips on the sensitive skin at the base of my throat. Her breath sending goosebumps down the back of my neck.

The hungry sound she made when I touched between her legs. God, she'd been so wet for me. It had been so easy between us. Felt so fucking right.

And I'd been enthralled with her. With every tiny whimper, with every stuttered breath as my lips moved over her chest, taking one perfect nipple in my mouth.

Then I'd laid her down on the pillow and knelt between her thighs... pushing into the tightest heat I'd ever felt ... my balls ache at the memory. Nothing had ever felt better. Yeah I'd been drunk, but I couldn't blame the alcohol. I knew exactly what I was doing. And besides, I'd been more drunk on her, on the pheromones, on the idea of being inside her than I had been on the alcohol I'd consumed.

But the look of hurt on her face the next morning was unmistakable. The way her lips trembled as she met my eyes. The way her hands curled into tense fists at her sides, and her mad rush to get away from me ...that's what fucking killed me. She got us coffee and food, and put on an Oscar-worthy performance of pretending the night before meant nothing. I didn't know what else to do besides follow her lead. I couldn't run the risk of making her feel more awkward around me than she already did.

And then later that day when I changed my sheets and found a few coin-sized spots of blood on the bedding... a fresh wave of confusion and emotion, and finally realization had gutted me all over again. I swallow down my anger, nostrils flaring even now. I still can't believe I let it get that far between us. That I took something from her that wasn't mine to take. I feel like complete scum right now.

I know I should apologize, or call her, or do something, but it's better if she just thinks I was too drunk to remember.

The guys around me erupt in laughter, and I realize Asher is still telling that goddamn story.

"She held her breath for like four minutes, dude. Swear to God!" he finishes, and the guys around us laugh. Teddy punches him in the shoulder and calls him an idiot.

Coach blows the whistle and we turn for the bench. I make a wide, lazy arc and take my time.

Part of me is relieved today's skate is done. But the other part of me knows I won't be able to avoid Owen any easier at home. Hopping over the wall, I grab a water bottle and I take a long drink.

When I got drafted, my life changed in an instant. Suddenly there were fans calling my name at every game, kids wearing my number on the back of their jerseys, and women in every city who wanted to fuck me, flashing perfect tits in my face, begging to come home with me.

Everyone wanted a piece of me. Everyone except for Owen and Elise. They were true friends. They were there before all this started. Owen and I had been playing hockey together on the frozen pond in our neighborhood since we were eight years old. Elise too.

I grin, remembering back to how we always made her play goalie because she was so horrible at it and we could score fifteen goals a game.

She was the one girl I could just be myself around. And now I've gone and fucked that up too. But what else could I do? I can't exactly apologize for sticking my dick in her, and taking something that wasn't mine to take. Because what's done is done. And I certainly can't confess my crime to her brother. So I'd ghosted. It's better this way. At least that's what I keep telling myself. It's not even a choice – even if I wanted to make something happen with Elise, my life is a shit show. I might have a kid on the way, for fuck's sake.

Letting her believe I was too drunk to remember what happened is the safer alternative for everyone involved. Because dealing with the fallout? It's not something I can handle. Owen's my best friend. My roommate. My teammate. And Elise is way too good for me. Nothing good could come from admitting we slept together.

"Hey, Brady, you okay?" Owen asks, stopping beside me.

I grab my towel from the bench and wipe the sweat from my face. "Just fucking great," I lie.

Inside the locker room, I strip down out of my equipment and take a lengthy shower. The hot water feels good on my aching muscles and I'm in no rush to leave the shower stall. I don't know how long it's going to take for the memories of Elise in my bed to fade, but I hope for my sake they do. The feel of her hands on my chest, memories of her huge blue-gray eyes peering up at mine as our bodies moved together …

I hope to God those memories fade. And not

because I want to forget, but because I can barely look Owen in the eye without admitting the whole thing to him. Eventually, the water cools and I have to shut it off and get out. Wrapping a towel around my hips I wander back to my locker, and find most of the guys are already dressed.

"Oh I almost forgot," Owen says, hoping up from the bench. He grabs a piece of paper from inside his gym bag and hands it to Asher, who's standing beside him in nothing but a pair of baggy sweatpants.

I push one hand through my damp hair and shake my head, already knowing where this is heading.

"What's this?" Asher asks, accepting the invoice and peering down at it.

"We had our hot tub serviced. This is the cleaning bill." Owen drops back onto the bench, satisfied with himself, and stuffs his feet into his shoes without bothering to untie them. "There was a thong clogging the filter," he adds at Asher's puzzled expression.

Asher lets out a grunt of surprise. "Two hundred bucks? The girl I was with wasn't wearing any panties. This is Teddy's bill. Here you go, TK.

That's all you." He hands the paper to Teddy, who looks down at it, brows creased.

On a roll now, Owen adds, "And you might want to consider some manscaping. There were pubes stuck in the drain and they charge extra for that."

"Manscaping? Do you even hear yourself?" Teddy asks, shaking his head. He turns from the locker and shoulders his bag..

It's a sad reality that I've seen these guys naked so many times I actually know their manscaping routines. *Fuck, that's just sad.*

"I'm serious, man. The chicks like it. You can't have hairy balls if you want them to be licked. That's just reality, bro." Owen shakes his head, face serious.

"You guys are disgusting animals, you know that right?" I ask.

"Yup," TK and Asher both answer at once.

Teddy crumples the paper up in his fist. "This is ridiculous. Let's call it even for all the beer you've snatched from my fridge."

Owen printed the invoice from his computer— even made the letterhead look like a legit cleaning company, so he doesn't put up a fight.

"You guys want to go eat?" Asher asks.

"Does a bear poop in the woods?" Owen replies, grinning.

I finish getting dressed quickly and follow them out of the building, hoping like hell I can survive the off-season without completely losing my shit.

CHAPTER SIX

My Own Personal Hell

Elise

Three Months Later

"You've got to be fucking kidding me," Owen calls, tossing the video game controller onto the couch and shaking his head. It's Sunday evening and I'm lounging across the gray sectional in my brother's penthouse apartment while he gets his ass handed to him on Xbox.

Justin, sitting on the couch opposite Owen and me, only chuckles. "Four to one, bro. You lost. *Again.*"

Owen picks up his bottle of beer from the coffee table in front of us and takes a long swig, draining it.

"Maybe if you had stayed out of the penalty

box a little more," Justin offers.

"Don't tell me how to do my job," Owen growls. He takes another sip, looking sullen. "You wanna play, Lise?"

I chuckle. He knows I'm God-awful at video ice hockey. "If you need someone to stroke your ego, you're going to have to find someone else."

Owen grins. "I want someone to stroke my---"

I hold up one hand, stopping him. "Let's keep this family-friendly."

"G-rated," Justin echoes, shooting me a sympathetic look.

It's taken me months, but I'm finally able to be in the same room as him and not want to cry. Or puke. *Yay, me.*

"You're dead to me, Brady." But Owen doesn't mean that. He's just pouting. They're like brothers, they're so close. It's disgusting how deep their codependence runs.

"Awe. Look who gets all crabby when he loses." Justin stands, stretching his arms over his head, making his t-shirt hitch up a couple of inches to reveal his defined set of abs.

Abs that no longer set my pulse on fire.

Okay, I'm lying. But hey, at least I'm trying to go through the motions. Even though I can still remember how those abs feel against my fingertips if I think about it long enough.

It's been three long months of trying to forget our night together, three months of pretending it never happened, and three months of wading through the kind of tough-love therapy that only your girlfriends can dish up. It didn't matter that that night in his bed left a permanent imprint on my heart. Didn't matter that Justin was still the only guy who sent my pulse into overdrive. I had moved on. I was dating someone new, and I was actively working on beating Justin at his game of pretending that night didn't exist. I wasn't very good at that game, but it didn't stop me from playing.

"Another beer?" Justin asks on his way to the kitchen.

"Abso-fuckin-lutely." Owen props his feet up on the coffee table. "You wanna come out with us tonight?" my brother asks, turning to meet my eyes and giving me his best puppy-dog stare.

"Not tonight," I say.

Justin returns with two bottles of beer and

hands one to Owen before twisting the cap off his own and taking a long sip.

I force my gaze away from watching the way his throat moves as he swallows.

"I'm staying in tonight," Justin says, setting the bottle down on the table. If I didn't know any better, it's almost like he's purposely avoiding looking at me. My brother hasn't noticed anything, but sometimes I catch Justin staring at me when no one else is looking.

I guess tonight is not one of those nights.

Owen flashes the sad puppy look at Justin. "It's been weeks since we've been out."

"Yeah but the season starts on Thursday. I want to lay low tonight."

"Two words. Lindsay and Lisbeth."

Justin rubs one hand over the back of his neck. "What about them?"

Owen laughs. "It's been two weeks. We should get out. Blow off some steam."

Justin gives me an uneasy look, but I'm suddenly really busy inspecting the polish on my thumbnail. If he thinks I don't know about all the puck bunnies, he's even more clueless than I thought. But it doesn't mean I want his sex life rubbed in my face. It's been hard enough watching him disappear from the bar early with a woman more times than I can count.

"Coach is going to be riding us hard. We can't be hungover tomorrow," Justin says.

Owen stays quiet, grabbing the video controller to start another game.

"Oh, now I've got your attention?" Justin chuckles.

"No. You've got my pity, dude. Two weeks without pussy? My balls would be officially blue," Owen says.

I force a smile and shake my head. Justin didn't say that it had been two weeks since he'd seen some action, just that it was two weeks ago since he and my brother went out with those twins—or Busty Barbie and Botox Betty as I like to call them.

And even though my heart is squeezing inside my chest at the thought of Justin with one of those girls, I laugh right along with Owen. I just hope he can't tell how hollow the sound is.

I took Becca's advice and moved on with my

life, but that doesn't mean I've gotten over what happened. I don't even know how that would be possible. Justin Brady has held a part of my heart since I was six years old. As I grew up, that comfortable fondness evolved from friendship into love…for me anyway.

The year I turned fourteen, Justin was away at college and wasn't at my birthday party like he usually would have been. And then to make matters worse, he decided to come home one weekend later when I was sick with the flu. He'd taken to staying at my parents' house rather than with his dad when he came back for a visit to avoid his family's nonstop drama. I didn't know all the specifics, I only knew that his dad had remarried and Justin didn't really feel welcome there anymore. Normally I'd be ecstatic to see him, but instead of spying on him and Owen and parading around in front of him in my best skinny jeans, I was laid up on the couch with a fever in my ratty bathrobe.

My mom kept trying to shoo everyone away from me so that no one else would get sick, but Justin would have none of that. He checked in on me several times, sitting with me to keep me company, and brought me tea when I complained of being freezing. I can still remember with clarity Owen shouting from the bedroom for Justin to re-join him in their video-game tournament, but Justin only grinned down at me, and called out to Owen the game could wait. That secret little smile meant the world to me. It still does. Even if I don't want it to.

So yeah, getting over our night of mind-blowing sex is probably not happening. Plus, to actually get over something, you probably have to, I don't know, talk about it like two grown ass adults. Which Justin and I never have. Without any type of closure my heart has remained wide open.

"Fine," Owen concedes. "Let's order some food. You in, Elise?"

"What?" I shake my head, tuning back into the conversation. "No, I already ate. And I'm going to get ice cream with Andy in a little while."

Owen abandons the game he's starting, and looks at me. "Damn. So it's getting pretty serious with this guy. Maybe I should meet him."

I can feel Justin watching us, but I don't meet his gaze.

"You will," I say to Owen. "Soon-ish."

The truth is, Andy's not a hockey fan, and I really can't imagine him getting along very well with my brother. When I told him my brother played pro-hockey, he made some offhand remark about hockey being little better than MMA with all the fighting. Hockey's always been a huge part of my life and while it's not a requirement that the person I'm dating be a fan, I'm not sure exactly how well ultra-conservative Andy and my foul-mouthed brother would get along.

I check the time on my phone and then rise to my feet. "Actually, I need to get going." I grab my purse, and slip on my jacket. Through the high-rise's floor-to-ceiling windows, I can see the light drizzle darkening the sky. It's officially fall in Seattle.

I lean down and give Owen a kiss on the cheek. "Goodnight. You two be good."

Before things went down between us, the old Justin would have made some flirty remark like, "I'm always good."

But now he stays quiet.

"Text me when you get home," Owen adds, eyes already back on the game.

I leave without a backward glance and make my way to the elevator at the end of the hall.

One day at a time.

Becca would be so proud.

• • •

I swirl my spoon through the melted puddle of chocolate ice cream in the bottom of my bowl.

"Did you hear what I said?" Andy asks, brows knitted in confusion as he looks at me.

"Hm? No, sorry."

He launches into some story about what happened in his third period class today, but I just can't get myself to focus. The fact that I'm a preschool teacher and he's a middle school math teacher should mean that we have something in common, only it's starting to feel less and less like we actually do.

I laugh when he's done talking and hope that I've read the social cues correctly. Andy balls up his napkin and tosses it inside his empty ice cream dish.

"You seem really distracted lately. Everything okay?" he asks.

He really is a sweet guy. Blond hair. Blue eyes.

Cute in a nerdy kind of way. I like him. At least, I think I do. Or maybe I just want to like him, or anyone other than Justin. I'm not even sure anymore.

I lean forward and press my lips to his, and will myself to feel something—anything as his kisses me back. I will my heart to beat faster, for my palms to get sweaty, for my nipples to tighten—anything.

Only none of that happens.

As I pull back and meet his eyes, Andy smiles.

He's a nice guy. But *nice* doesn't set my skin on fire, doesn't make my belly fill with butterflies like Justin does. I don't feel like I'm going to die if he doesn't get his hands on me in the next four seconds.

And none of that is Andy's fault, but fuck. I hate this.

I'm pretty sure Justin's dick broke me, and I don't know if I'll ever be fixed.

CHAPTER SEVEN

Douchebags

Justin

A plate of cold pizza sits on the coffee table in front of me. I'd lost my appetite about the time Elise announced that it was getting serious between her and the guy she's been dating. She left an hour ago and Owen called some of the guys over. I've been watching them play video games, but I couldn't tell you who won or lost, or what any of the trash talk over the past hour has entailed.

Just the thought of her with someone else brings out all my protective, caveman instincts. Fuck, it's not like I've been a saint—far from it—but hooking up with someone I won't ever see again feels a hell of a lot different than Elise developing feelings for someone she's in a relationship with. *I sound like such a hypocrite. Correction, I am a hypocrite.*

"Brady!" Teddy calls from the other side of the room. He's waving a video game controller in the air to get my attention.

"Pull your tampon out and play me," he says with a challenging smirk.

I flash him my middle finger, but take the controller that Asher offers over from beside me.

He's right though, I am distracted. And I really don't want my team to notice, because I'm not in a position to answer any questions, especially not with Owen sitting on the other end of the couch.

"Get ready to get annihilated," I say, flashing him a cocky grin.

"You've been playing like shit all night, there's no way you're going to beat me," he mutters.

And … Apparently he was right, because three games later, I hand over the controller in defeat.

No one else comments on my funk of a mood though.

"Dude, it's not the playoffs, it's time to shave the vagina growing on your face," Teddy says to Owen, shaking his head.

I glance over at Owen and can't help but

chuckle. He's pouting out his lips and damn if I'm not picturing another set of pink lips surrounded by stubble. I shudder. That's not a mental image you want associated with your best friend.

Fuck. What I need is another beer.

Or a lobotomy to get that visual out of my brain.

"Go ahead, TK. Keep being a dick," Owen says to Teddy, "and I won't share the girls I just texted."

"Ah, come on, fucker. Don't be like that," Teddy groans. "You know you love me."

"You got bunnies coming over?" Asher asks.

I side-eye him, remembering all the times he's desecrated the hot tub on our balcony. I wish he'd just take one the fuck home. I'm not in the mood for their shit tonight. "Yup. Got a group of girls coming by," Owen confirms. "Brady needs to get some. He's been in a funk ever since training camp ended."

I guess he did notice. I shrug and lean my head back against the cushion. "I'm not in a funk. I just don't like the off-season as much as you bastards seem to. Glad it's over."

Somehow Owen has a way of turning a quiet night at home playing video games into a chance for him to hookup. The dude's a major manwhore, and that's saying something coming from me. But Owen just takes it to a whole new level.

I wander into the kitchen and help myself to another bottle of beer, popping the top off and taking a deep swig as I rest one hip against the counter. I'm really not in the mood for our place to turn into a party pad tonight.

Owen enters the kitchen to grab a drink for himself and stops to appraise me. "You alright, man?"

I nod, and take another sip. "Just fucking peachy." I force a fake smile.

Owen rolls his eyes. "You know I can see straight through you."

I shrug. "Just got a lot on my mind."

He twists off the top of his beer and tosses it across the room where it lands inside the trash can. "Not the chick from South Carolina, I hope."

"It was Tennessee, and nope. I haven't given her a second thought."

Okay that's not exactly the truth. That situation was one of the reasons I started looking at casual hookups differently.

Owen knows the full sordid story. When I found out I had a kid on the way, of course I'd confided in my best friend. Shit, I'd been scared out of my mind.

I'd flown to Nashville and then rented a car to make the trip to her place. We'd kept in touch pretty much daily since she told me she was pregnant. We weren't together, but that didn't stop me from checking on her, asking about the baby, or sending money for the things she said she needed. I had mentally prepared myself to be part of this child's life, no matter what happened, but when I showed up on her doorstep, all of that unraveled. Quickly.

She answered the door stumbling and slurring her words. It didn't take long to figure out she'd been drinking, and she was stick-thin. She certainly didn't look seven months pregnant like she had claimed. When I pressed her for the truth, she started crying and admitted everything.

After an entire day spent travelling, the whole time feeling equal parts terrified but determined that I was going to be a good father, only to find that she had lied to me, I left there in a fog. I spent a sleepless night in a cheap motel by the airport since I couldn't get a flight out until the following morning. I'd envisioned assembling a crib and painting walls, and maybe getting to listen to the baby's heartbeat … instead all my life choices suddenly hit me at full force. I laid on a lumpy mattress listening to highway traffic and started to wonder if there was more out there than just meaningless sex.

Owen clears his throat, and I realize he's still watching me.

I lick my lips and cross one ankle over the other. "So, this guy Elise is seeing. What do you know about him?"

Owen shrugs. "He's a teacher. Treats her well, she says. I haven't met the dude yet, but I intend to."

It stings to hear him say this. Of course I want her to be treated well, but most of me hoped to hear him say that the guy was a douchebag. And then what? We hatch a plan to go over to her apartment and get her to break up with this guy? Fuck. This isn't high school anymore.

I know I missed my shot with her, but that doesn't make the thought of her with someone else sting any less. I've had a crazy run over the past few months and my emotions are all over the fucking place.

I give a half nod. "Just want to make sure she's

being treated right."

Owen looks over at me, his eyes tracking the movement of my beer to my lips as he watches me. "Elise can handle herself. She wouldn't do anything stupid."

I nod. She can handle herself. I remember that all too well. The way her hands had clamped down on my naked ass to tug me closer, the way she ground her pelvis against mine, seeking her release. The breathy gasps she made into my neck when she came.

I swallow and look down at the bottle I'm gripping way too tightly in my fist. "Yeah, she's a smart girl," I manage at last. I need to close my damn mouth before I say something I shouldn't.

Owen nods, and wanders back to the living room—thank God, because I'm not sure how much longer I can go on with this charade.

I know I don't deserve a girl like her, I fuck up everything I touch, but that doesn't stop me from wanting Elise. I still hate myself that I never found a way to apologize for that night, and make it right. Although I'm not sure there is a way to make it right when you drunkenly take your teammate's little sister to bed.

A little while later, the girls arrive. Kaitlyn, Kirsten and something else with a K that I already forgot. I'm so not in the mood for this shit, and when they talk the girls into playing strip poker, I head out onto the balcony with my beer and my somber thoughts, just wanting to be alone.

The cool, dark air fits my mood perfectly. Part of me wants to text Elise and check on her, but the rest of me knows that would be a terrible idea. We've barely exchanged three sentences since that night. I can't exactly strike up a conversation out of the blue just because I'm jealous that she's seeing someone. She's going exactly what she should do be doing—moving on with her life.

The balcony door slides open and one of the girls saunters out. Kaitlyn I think, but fuck, I'm not sure.

"Hey," she says, her voice small. "Thought you could use some company out here." She wanders closer, watching me.

"You're not much for strip poker?" I ask.

She sits down next to me, folding her legs beneath her and hugging her arms around her chest. It's cold out here, and she's not exactly dressed for the weather in leggings and a thin t-shirt. "I suck at poker," she says, eyes meeting mine.

I inhale slowly, then bring my beer to my lips, taking a long drink.

"So what position do you play?" she asks.

"Forward," I say, still looking out at the city skyline. One thing I love about Elise. We never talk hockey. I smile at the realization. It's a huge part of my life, and Elise gets that, but we never bother with the mundane chit-chat about it because she's been there for the whole ride.

"That means you try to score," she says with a smile. I appreciate a good double entendre as much as the next guy, but tonight I can't find it in me to smile back.

"That's the idea." I take another sip, looking out at the skyline, and it's quiet for a moment.

"You must love it," she says.

"Yeah, I do. I've been playing since I was four."

I'm just waiting for her to make some comment about how I'm good with my stick or some other euphemism I've heard eight thousand times before, but instead she places one hand on my thigh and leans closer. "It's kind of chilly out here. If you wanted to go inside, maybe just to talk, I'd be okay with that."

I glance over and meet her eyes. It's dark out so I can't see their color, just the heavy makeup she's wearing. For a split-second I consider her offer. I could fuck Elise out of my memory. She'd been the last girl in my bed. I've messed around a little, but I haven't brought anyone else to my bed. And this girl sitting beside me … She's pretty, she seems nice enough, and she's clearly into me, that much is obvious. And yet I have zero interest in her.

There's not so much as a twitch of interest in my pants.

"I'm sorry," I mutter. "I'm not in the mood tonight."

"I'm not actually here to seduce you. You just seemed sad."

"That's… kind of you. But I'm okay, I've just got a lot on my mind."

Kaitlyn, or whatever her name is nods, but she seems unconvinced.

"Have a good night," I say, standing.

Without waiting for her response, I trudge across the balcony and head inside.

When I pull the sliding door open and walk inside, it's to the sound of laughter.

"Damn, that was fast champ!" Asher calls.

"Minute man," Teddy coughs into his fist.

I don't correct them, I just continue in a straight line to my bedroom and close the door.

Inside, I lean both hands against my dresser and draw a deep breath. I desperately need things to go back to normal. My sanity depends on it. We've got a huge season ahead of us, and I need to be playing my best if we're going to follow up our performance from last season where we took home the championship title. I can't allow Elise, or who she's dating, to get in the way of that. It's time to let her move on… so I can also move on.

CHAPTER EIGHT

Dumplings

Elise

"**E**xcellent work," I say, bending down to inspect the finger-painting mess my eight toddlers are currently making at the table. There are yellow suns and red flowers, and a whole lot of brownish squiggly smears.

And despite the sheer craziness of arts and crafts time, I really am proud of them. I love being a preschool teacher. From nine to four every day, I'm responsible for eight little people who completely adore me. I'm greeted with hugs in the morning, I get the honor of bandaging scraped knees and soothing hurt feelings, and there's usually someone who tells me I'm pretty. All in all, it's not a bad workday. Plus, we get snack time. I'm all about snack time. Today we had animal crackers. They're my secret weapon when I really need the kids to listen.

"Look at mine, Miss Lise!" Carter calls out—completely forgetting the lesson I taught him on using his inside voice.

I kneel down so we're at eye level. "It's wonderful," I say in a low voice. "I can tell you worked very hard."

He beams up at me. "I sure did."

"Mommy's going to have something beautiful to decorate her fridge."

I grin as I move across the room to help the children place their masterpieces in the drying rack. I love these little humans. I mean, yeah they're like mini crazy drunk people, but I adore them all the same.

I'm completely in my element managing the chaos of removing eight tiny smocks, and supervising the washing of sixteen little hands, and not even the text I got earlier can dampen my mood. Which is strange considering the contents of said text message. And yeah, it's probably a bit alarming, but I literally felt nothing when I looked down at the words Andy sent to me earlier.

He'd broken up with me over text, saying he

thought we'd be better off as friends. I'd replied with the thumbs up emoji. If that doesn't tell you how broken I am, nothing will. It might have set the world record for the world's fastest—and least engaging—breakup.

But I'd texted Becca and she rounded up the girls, and so tonight after work, we're meeting for happy hour at one of my favorite places. The guys have practice tonight, and so I haven't told Owen about my breakup with Andy yet, but it's hardly front page news. Yeah, I'd dated him for a couple of months, but I'm hardly upset about it. But that doesn't mean I won't let my girlfriends spoil me with cocktails and appetizers tonight.

• • •

"A round of shots?" Sara asks, eyebrows raised in concern across the table.

I set my menu down and shake my head. "It's not that kind of a breakup."

"Are you denying us a perfectly good reason to drink?" Sara is a couple of years older, the same age as my brother and Justin, and she's an attorney. "Fine, we'll celebrate then. To being young, single and open to new adventures."

Becca is seated beside me, with Sara and Bailey across from us.

"That'll work. I just want something yummy that will numb my brain." I glance at the drink specials again.

"Something numby then. Coming right up." Not one to wait around for our server to show up, Sara marches up to the bar to put our order in.

We're seated near the bay windows and the setting sun and the gray drizzle makes me want to curl up in a cozy sweater and drink hot chocolate, but gossiping and drinking cocktails with my girlfriends is a very close second. I'd asked Becca not to say anything to the girls after my night with Justin. I didn't think I could handle three sets of sad eyes peering at me with pity. And I'm thankful she's kept it to herself. Losing your virginity to someone who doesn't even remember it isn't exactly a high point in life.

We're halfway through our first round when the server finally comes over to check on us. Becca promptly orders half a dozen appetizers, including the steamed dumplings I love, while Sara gets us another round of drinks.

I love my friends.

We trade stories about our workdays, and Becca supplies gossip from the hockey team. She works as an assistant to the team owner and always has the best gossip. Apparently last season's rookie was released during the off-season for boinking the coach's daughter. Whoops. Way to fuck up your pro-career in three seconds flat, buddy.

We're all pleasantly buzzed when the atmosphere in the bar suddenly shifts. Hushed whispers fall over the tables surrounding us and my eyes swing over to the doors just in time to see four hulking hockey players entering the bar. It's my brother and Justin flanked by Teddy and Asher. These guys would cause a stir wherever they go—they're young, fit and attractive, but in this city, they're practically gods. Being professional athletes and part of a popular winning team will do that I guess.

I hadn't known to expect them, but this bar is near the rink. I guess they're grabbing a drink after practice.

Becca half stands and waves them over and the guys get busy pulling another table up to join ours. "I texted Owen that we were here," she says. And then she meets my eyes. "Oh."

Yeah. *Oh.* I know Becca and Owen are good friends, but she should have realized that inviting him here meant Justin would most likely tag along.

My eyes make a greedy sweep of his tall frame without my brain's permission. His denim clad thighs are muscular and powerful and his long-sleeve t-shirt stretches tautly across his broad chest. He could pass for a superhero. Or maybe he's the villain?

It doesn't matter how attractive he is. He's broken and I need to move on. Period, end of story.

I've gotten really good at avoiding him, and when he takes a seat at the opposite end of the table, I release the little breath I'd been holding.

The guys order drinks and our appetizers are delivered.

"To Andy, the douche, for freeing Elise up so she can move on to bigger and better things in her future…" Becca says, hiccupping a little at the end of her toast.

We clink glasses and everyone drinks except for me. I'm too busy figuring out how to discreetly kick Becca under the table.

My brother meets my eyes across the table. "You broke up?"

I shrug, and open my mouth to respond just as

Becca leans forward.

"He dumped her. Via text message," she says, a little too loudly. "What kind of a garbage person does that?"

Sara shakes her head and slides Becca's drink away from her. "Jesus, Becs. I'm cutting you off."

My cheeks burn with the attention of the entire table now looking at me—notably Justin. His blue gaze feels hot and makes me jittery like there's suddenly a million butterflies dancing the cha-cha inside my stomach. *Ignore it*, my brain demands.

I raise my martini glass and take a sip of the potent cocktail. "Nothing a little alcohol can't fix." I force a fake grin. And then my eyes meet Justin's across the table. That was a bad idea. He looks so intense and serious. And he's frowning at me. His hair is still slightly damp from the shower, and God, I'd give anything to smell him. Which is fucked up, I know that. But the heart wants what it wants, and mine stupidly still wants him.

Even after everything that's happened. Or shit, maybe it's because of everything that's happened, hell I don't know. Or maybe Andy breaking up with me out of the blue hit me harder than I thought. I force my eyes away from Justin's and bring my drink to my lips, only to discover it's already gone.

When did that happen?

Justin raises one hand, summoning the waitress to return, I hear him ordering another drink. There's only a glass of ice water in front of him, but he tips his chin toward me and the perky waitress nods. Then he orders another plate of dumplings, instructing her to deliver them to me. What the hell? Why is he being so nice to me when he's avoided me like the plague the entire summer?

Actually let's not get carried away. *Nice* is a relative term. The dude hasn't said more than half a dozen words to me in the months since we slept together. It's a freaking miracle that Owen hasn't noticed. Of course we act the part well, we laugh at all the right times, and take all the good natured ribbing as though nothing has changed between us. Then again, maybe Justin really doesn't remember. Maybe he's not pretending at all. Maybe it's just me.

A few minutes later, a fresh cocktail appears in front of me and Justin watches me take my first sip. My hands are shaky and it has zero to do with the alcohol I've already consumed. It's with great effort that I set the glass back down without any of the contents sloshing over the side. Next, a steaming plate of dumplings appears at the table, and Justin has to bat the hands away from them.

"Hands off, fuckers. Those are for Elise."

I accept the plate he passes down the table. The guys did polish off most of the appetizers we ordered. But still, Justin remembered these were my favorite.

"Thanks," I murmur weakly, not wanting to make a big deal of his thoughtful gesture.

I'm sure it's just a case of him wanting to be nice to the girl who just got her heart broken. Only my heart's broken for him and not Andy, but I can't say that. Only Becca knows the truth.

She helps herself to one of my dumplings and smiles. "That was awfully sweet of Justin."

I elbow her in the ribs under the table and force a smile. She gets a little too chatty when she's drunk and I cannot afford to have something slip out of her mouth unwarranted.

But she's right. I can't help but wonder about his intentions. Is it really just because I got dumped or is it because he does remember what happened that night and feels badly?

"Owen seems to be enjoying himself," Becca

says, nodding once to my brother as he meets her eyes and smiles.

"He usually does," I murmur.

That's a true statement. My brother can find joy in the most mundane moments. I'm pretty sure going to the dentist's office with my brother would be fun. Scratch that, I know it is. He kept me entertained throughout our entire childhood.

Normally the talk turns to hockey with our group, but tonight Bailey, Owen and Asher are in some deep conversation about which movies from our childhood were the best.

"Harry Potter," I shout to a chorus of groans.

"God, you're so young, Elise," Sara says.

I roll my eyes. Most of our group is in their late twenties while I just turned twenty-four a few weeks ago. "Whatever."

"Mary Poppins is my jam," Becca announces.

"The remake or the original?" Owen asks.

She plants one hand over her heart in mock disgust. "The original."

"Mary Poppins was hot," Asher adds, agreeing with her, but for entirely the wrong reason.

Becca laughs beside me.

"Hey, Becca," my brother calls down to our end of the table. "You hear about the rookie?" He's grinning.

"Yup. Crash and burn." She makes a blowing up motion with her hands.

Trading insider gossip is their currency. The juicier the better. I'm really glad that Becca has my brother. She's been through a lot, and he's like a big brother to her too.

After another round, I've gotten tipsier than expected and I suddenly stand. "I need to get home. I have to teach preschool in the morning."

"So responsible," Sara mutters. "And I better go too. I've gotta lawyer it up in court tomorrow." She stands, grabbing her purse from the back of the chair. "Want to share an Uber?"

Justin rises to his feet. "I can take Elise. Splitting an Uber doesn't work—she lives on the other side of town."

Owen looks at him curiously. "You've only had water, right?"

Justin nods. "Yeah, I'm good."

Apparently the fate of my journey home has been decided. Owen nods his consent and Justin rises, fishing his car keys out from the pocket of his dark jeans.

I rise on shaky legs, suddenly wishing I hadn't drank quite so much, and lean down to give Owen a kiss on the cheek. "Night," I murmur. "Make sure Becca gets home safe."

"Will do," Owen says, and then he flashes a pointed look at Justin. "Be careful with my little sister, she's precious cargo."

Justin looks directly at him, communicating something I don't understand. "I know, don't worry. I won't let anything bad happen to her."

Owen nods. "I've got her tab."

Becca—God bless her, she is the world's worst drunk person—leans over to me and whispers loudly, "You okay? This could be a good thing, right?"

I nod tightly, and dart away, terrified of what else she might *whisper-yell* in my direction.

As I follow Justin to the door, part of me thinks Becca could be right. It might be good for us to talk. It's been months, we need to clear the air at some point. Don't we?

Even if I want to be mad at him, part of me still misses his friendship.

As I follow him to the car, I'm transported back to one of the many times Justin came to my rescue.

I had just turned fifteen, and was out on my first date, unbeknownst to my parents. Gabe was a sophomore, and I was a freshman. He had his own car, and I thought he was the coolest, hottest guy in school. He wasn't anywhere near Justin-level hotness, but since Justin had yet to notice that I was growing up, I had to take what I could get. Gabe and I went to a party, and unfortunately for me, he'd started drinking. The longer the night wore on, the more my anxiety started to grow. I knew I couldn't get in the car with him later, which meant I had no way to get home. Since I was afraid to call Owen, I did the next best thing. I called Justin and he was there within fifteen minutes, hauling Gabe outside and ripping him a new one. He was so intense, so angry, but also so sweet with me. I recall the way his fingers trembled as he buckled me into the passenger seat.

Blinking away the memory, I climb into the black SUV beside him. Just before he closes my door, his eyes meet mine, and I swear I see in them the same look he gave me that night we had sex.

But then the door shuts and he walks around to his side of the car.

"Buckle up." His tone is neutral, but a little guarded and I have the strangest feeling he's upset about something.

He pulls onto the road, and the silence stretches between us. It's tense, and awkward. We never used to be like this. God, why did I agree to come with him? Oh yeah because I'm drunk and I have no self-control when it comes to Justin Fucking Brady.

"Talk to me E," he finally says, fingers curling around the steering wheel.

"What do you want to talk about?" I try to keep my tone casual, but I'm terrified that I know exactly what he wants to talk about.

"It's just... shouldn't we clear the air?"

"About?" I blink at him.

He's going to have to spell it out for me. I'm done assuming where this man is concerned. I assumed he was into me that night, but I clearly read that wrong. And I won't repeat the same mistake twice.

"Oh, I don't know. How about that time you

woke up in my bed naked?" His deep voice hits me straight in the chest.

"If you've got something to say, say it." My tone is firm as feelings that have been buried for months rise to the surface.

He waits at the light, making a left-hand turn without saying anything just yet.

Well that's just fucking perfect. "It's fine, Justin. We don't have to talk about anything." I lean my head back against the headrest and close my eyes while my heart hammers out an uneven rhythm in my chest.

CHAPTER NINE

Broken Hearts and Broken Promises

Justin

Well this is an interesting turn of events. My current status? I have a drunk Elise sitting next to me in the cab of my dark SUV as we cruise toward her apartment across town.

Elise, resting her head against the headrest, inhales audibly, letting her breath out slowly. "It smells like you in here."

I make a confused face. "Ah … my hockey bag's in the back, so I'm guessing that's not a compliment." Hockey equipment is about the worst smelling thing you can imagine, and I'm about to mutter an apology when she shakes her head.

"No. It smells like your cologne. Hermès Woods, right?"

I nod. How the fuck does she know what kind of cologne I wear?

I tighten my grip on the steering wheel.

She stares out the window, lost in thought while I focus on *not fucking crashing the car.* This is a bit surreal being alone with her after all this time, and Owen's words of warning ring through my head.

I've been half hard since she followed me out of the bar, as if my dick remembers the last time we were alone together, and he's ready to be moved from the bench and be put in the game. And the fact that she's still sitting there breathing in my scent like it's her own personal version of heaven isn't helping things.

Us alone together plus alcohol was how everything got so fucked up last time. I can't let myself repeat our mistakes. I just told her brother that I wouldn't let anything bad happen to her. And I'm every form of bad that could possibly happen to her. But damn if I don't like having her close. I'm tempted to slow the car just to draw out my time with her. Weird, I know.

Satisfied with the radio station she's found, she stops fiddling with the controls and sits back in her seat, hands resting on her thighs.

"So this breakup…" I attempt small talk. "You okay?"

She takes a deep breath and shakes her head. "I'm fine. And you don't have to pretend you're worried about me."

Pretend? Is she high right now?

I know full well that I'm responsible for some, fuck *most*, of the turmoil in her life over the past few months, and I hate the thought that I'm responsible for this too.

She's the one bright spot in my life, and I can't handle knowing she's sad. I would make it my personal mission in life to make her happy if I could. Especially since I know I'm at least partly responsible for her heartbreak.

I pull the car to the side of the road, and turn to face her, hands still gripping the wheel so I don't do anything stupid like reach over and touch her.

"I'm not pretending, Elise. I care about you. I always have. Now let's try this again. Are you okay?" I enunciate each word slowly, letting them sink in.

She bites her lower lip and nods, those huge gray eyes locked on mine. "I'm okay."

It doesn't escape my notice that she doesn't say I'm good, or I'm great, or I'm fine. She's *okay*. I need her to be a hell of a lot better than okay. But at least she's talking to me. It's a start, I guess.

I inhale deeply and pull the car back onto the road after checking my mirrors. She smells so good. Like body wash and Elise—like fresh air and sunshine, and those lemon cocktails she had. Fuck, I want to kiss her.

Instead, I start rambling. "I never met the guy, but for what it's worth, your brother said you were way too good for him."

Elise grins. "Did he now?"

I nod. "Yeah. And he said that the dude was a douche canoe." Owen did not say that, but you can't make me take it back for all the money in the world, not with the way Elise lets out a giggle and covers her mouth with her hand. That sound leaving her lips dissolves all the tension in the car.

"Thanks, Justin."

I swallow down a strange wave of emotion. Man, it feels so good just to be here with her in this moment, talking, laughing. God, I've fucking missed this. I've missed her friendship more than anything. It's taken me this exact moment with her laughing beside me to realize just how much I've missed it. I have so many regrets, but losing her as a friend is definitely the biggest.

Our moment over, I focus on the road and getting Elise home safe. It's the least I can do.

"Oh my God, Taco Casa! We have to stop!" Elise calls out beside me, pointing to the neon-lit sign of the fast food restaurant up ahead.

I chuckle and slow the car, pulling into the parking lot at her command.

"Thank you," she groans. "I never had dinner. I need something more than those dumplings to soak up all this alcohol if I'm going to be teaching America's youth in the morning."

I shake my head, and chuckle again, pulling up to the window to order. "Yeah, I'm starved too."

Elise gives me her order, and I double everything, right down to the hot sauce and iced tea.

She smiles at me, and shyly tucks her hair behind one ear. Something about that strikes me. She was never shy around me before.

After we order our food, I insist on paying, and then we drive to her place. When we pull up out front, Elise turns to me.

"You want to come inside and eat?"

I know I should say no. There are literally ten thousand reasons why this would be a terrible idea. But tonight's the first time I've seen her laugh in months. If she's nursing a broken heart, I should be there to cheer her up, right? Or make sure she doesn't choke on her food. Damn, the lies I'm willing to tell myself are getting a little ridiculous—even for me.

Yet I follow her inside, carrying the bag of tacos while she holds onto the cups of iced tea. Her place is cute and really girly. I've been here once or twice with Owen. It's much cleaner than our bachelor pad. It smells a lot better too. There's a pink and orange rug in a sunburst pattern under her gray couch and framed photos on the walls of her family. My gaze lingers on the picture of her parents, smiling at each other. Together we head to the couch and each unwrap a taco.

At the first bite, Elise lets out a soft groan. "Oh my God, why are these so good?"

I take a bite of my own and wipe my mouth with one of the two thousand napkins they gave us. "It's fucking amazing. You know what this reminds me of?"

She squints at me, but shakes her head.

My lips twitch with a smile. "My senior year of high school. You were, God, you were what, in eighth grade?"

She nods, and takes another small bite, still watching me.

"Owen and I skipped practice to smoke weed, and we got a whole bunch of tacos and hung out in your parents' basement all afternoon."

She must remember the day I'm referring to, because suddenly she starts laughing behind a napkin.

"Your parents got home from work and ..."

She stops me, raising one hand, still chuckling. "And I immediately told on you guys. I never said sorry for that, did I?"

I shake my head. "It's all good, E-class. I've never held it against you. Even though I got grounded for like a month after that."

Elise looks away from me and takes a long drink of her iced tea, setting down her half-eaten taco on its paper wrapper. "I'm feeling a lot better thanks to this greasy goodness. Tomorrow I can face my students hangover free. Thanks, Justin."

"No problem." I finish my food, and wipe my hands on the napkin. It grows quiet between us, and I'm not sure if I should go or what. But fuck, I'm not ready to leave.

She tucks her hair behind one ear, looking contemplative. God, that hair. Those silky dark waves. I remember exactly what it feels like when my fingers are threaded through it. I remember the smell of her shampoo and how it felt dragging over my chest when she kissed a path along my neck.

I clear my throat, forcing the thoughts away. "You sure you're okay about the breakup?"

She nods. "I'm sure. Thanks though. Sweet of you to ask." She gives me a half-smile, but I'll take it. She hasn't smiled at me in so long.

But sweet? Me? Yeah, no. Sweet is not an adjective I'd use to describe a guy who takes the v-card of a girl he's known all of his life and then disappears like a coward. That's the exact fucking opposite of *sweet*. A jerkface is more like it.

"What about you?" Elise asks, drawing me from my thoughts.

"What about me?" Is she seriously asking if I'm dating anyone? Isn't the answer to that question obvious? I don't date. I fuck around. Isn't that what everyone expects anyway?

Elise bites her lip and takes another sip of her drink. "Your relationship status … Still loving the bachelor lifestyle?"

I consider her question for a moment. The media blows my love-life out of proportion. I never thought Elise of all people would buy into the hype. But I like that she's actually asking me directly and not assuming like everyone else does.

But Elise also knows the shit-storm of my parents' divorce, and how it's made me gun-shy about relationships.

"I guess I just haven't found the right girl yet. And even though I've never been the relationship-type, part of me wonders if maybe it's time to grow up." I don't mean to be so honest with her, but I'm not lying. It's not something I've ever had before, but that doesn't mean I don't want it.

I can't tell if my response surprises her, but she doesn't say anything else. And I know I should, but I can't make myself get up and go just yet. Instead I do the one thing I know I shouldn't, I move closer to her on the couch.

Huge gray eyes look up at mine, and fuck, I'm done. I'm done resisting this girl, with her sweet personality and her quick wit. I'm all wrong for her, but she's gorgeous and I want this. So fucking badly. Or maybe I just want redemption. Either way, I can't go on like this.

She doesn't want to talk about what happened, but I'm more of a take action kind of guy anyway.

I lower my mouth toward hers and Elise parts her lips as my mouth meets hers in a slow, tentative kiss.

Her shaky breath ghosts over my lips as I go back in for more, deepening our connection and coaxing her tongue out to touch mine.

Fuck. It's electric. I stifle a groan and thread my fingers in the hair at the back of her neck.

She kisses me back and I'm in heaven. The taste of her, the softness of her lips eagerly moving under mine, brings me right back to the first night we kissed in my bedroom. The quiet sounds she makes, the feel of her trembling fingers skimming along my chest…nothing has ever felt more right. I feel so many things in this moment, I can't even put it into words. The rush of adrenaline. An intense pressure in my groin. She's kissing me. Open mouthed and hungry. I stroke her tongue with mine, and she makes a low sound in her throat. The noise is something in between a moan and a sigh of relief, and the skin on the back of my neck tingles.

But then, two firm hands are pushing against my chest.

I stop immediately and put some space between us. The air around us is charged with pheromones and desire and I miss the warmth of her body heat close to mine, but I have no other choice than to respect her need for space.

My eyes meet hers, trying to read what she's thinking. I would never want her to feel threatened or unsure about the physical contact between us. But even as I meet her eyes, I come up blank.

"We can't," she says, breathless. Her fingers touch her lips and her eyes are two huge pools of worry.

My heart stops and I give her a shaky nod. "I know."

I should regret pushing her into a kiss, but I don't. It's never been about winning with her, and I'm not playing a game. All I need is one more shot at redemption, and I'm determined to get it.

CHAPTER TEN

Admissions of Guilt

Elise

He kissed me. *Justin Brady was kissing me.*

On my couch.

I'm trying to remember how we arrived at this exact moment. One minute we were eating tacos and talking casually, and then the next his mouth was devouring mine.

My lips tingle with the hint of spice and the last thing I wanted to do was tell him to stop, even though I know with certainty it was the right call.

"E-Class," he murmurs, voice a little strained.

While my confused brain is still trying to work out if maybe he's actually interested in me, my lips start moving.

"What are we doing?" I hear myself ask him.

I want to slap a hand over my mouth, but then I see Justin thoughtfully weighing my question, and now I want nothing more than to hear his response. I practically hold my breath while I wait for it.

"I don't know. But I'm attracted to you, and I think you're attracted to me."

Oh. Well then. He's not wrong about that last part, but this isn't a conversation I ever imagined having with him.

Why did he kiss me? Had he thought about kissing me since that night? Did he want to make me smile? So many conflicting theories run through my brain.

Still, I remain speechless, waiting.

"I guess I just wanted to cheer you up." His smirk is so deliciously sexy that I have to physically stop myself from pouncing on him. I can think of about a dozen ways he could cheer me up. I could probably even invent a few more.

But then my libido takes a backseat, and my brain kicks back on. I've been replaying in my head how this conversation would go for the past three months, and I won't miss my opportunity.

Not now. I can't. I couldn't live with myself if I didn't address the elephant in the room. I take a deep breath and meet his eyes. "You really don't remember what happened between us do you? The night you guys beat Detroit in game seven last season ..."

He looks down at the ground between our feet. "Yeah," his voice comes out strained. "I remember."

Wait. What?

Hold up. That morning he acted like nothing had happened... I felt so used and alone. Like I was just a meaningless hookup he invited to his bed. Another woman to add to his list of conquests. It was awful. Beyond awful. I'd been in agony since that night. So angry and filled with such regret.

"*You ... remember?*"

"Fuck." When he looks up at me, his eyes are filled with his own regrets. A freaking mountain of them. "I've felt like shit for that for three months, two weeks and ..." He takes a second to think, eyes searching mine. "Four days."

A little pang of emotion hits me straight in the chest. He needs to start making sense. Right the fuck now.

"But I didn't know what else to do," he continues. "God, the look on your face the morning after. It was obvious you regretted it. I didn't want to put you in a weird position with your brother. I thought I was doing the right thing. I was trying to protect you, Elise."

I make a small noise of annoyed disagreement, wanting to point out that I'm an adult and I don't need protecting. Instead, I inhale and rub one hand over my face. I'm honestly speechless. He'd pretended not to know we had sex. Is that worse than actually forgetting?

I shake my head, still processing. "I… You… What?" I inhale, and am searching for something to say when Justin continues.

"I remember, okay? All of it. Every whimper, every moan, every pant. How perfectly we moved together. How you taste, how your body felt around mine, how soft you felt beneath me. Shit, I remember every-fucking-thing. And I can't seem to get you out of my head." His voice is so desperate and gravelly, it pierces straight through my heart.

That makes two of us.

But I won't give him the satisfaction of knowing that.

I want to be mad at him. I want to yell and scream and curse at him. But instead I just feel sad. Empty. Like we wasted the last three months tip-toeing around this. Avoiding each other. I've wasted months feeling awful about that night. We used to be friends, almost like family and now I feel so strange in his presence, like there's this huge messy thing stretching out between us.

Justin shoves one hand in his pocket and gives me a sorrow filled look. "I figured I had messed up so bad, it was better if we both moved on and forgot it ever happened. It was a mistake, right? Us hooking up?"

"This isn't like when we were kids. You don't have to treat me like I'm about to break."

My brain is working overdrive when Justin suddenly stands up to leave. "I'm sorry, I should go."

He can't go. I stand and do the only thing I can think of. I grab him by the front of his shirt, holding him close. I'm not sure whether to slap him, or kiss him, and the indecision has me paralyzed. What happens next, no matter which outcome, will change the course of our friendship completely.

It's then I realize that I'm shaking. My entire

body is trembling, and I have no idea why. Maybe it's because three months of feeling like a miserable piece of shit is a long time and between the break up and the alcohol and the kissing, I feel emotionally exhausted and confused.

"Hey, it's okay. Breathe for me."

I draw a slow, shuddering inhale.

Justin continues gazing at me with that curious, watchful stare I can't decipher. "Let's sit down."

He lowers us to the couch and his fingers gently touch the back of my neck, caress along my jawline, and raw emotion riots inside me.

I don't want him saying sweet things to me or kissing me like he can't bear the thought of his lips not touching mine.

I need him to keep pretending that night never happened—that I mean nothing to him. Less than nothing. My heart won't be able to take him being sweet to me. I know we don't have a future, I've accepted that. And broken, manwhore Justin Brady looking at me with heat in his eyes will only lead to trouble. *Won't it?*

I try to conjure Becca's voice, her dire warnings but I come up blank, because I remember that she invited Owen to the bar, knowing that Owen always has his shadow with him. The shadow that's now sitting beside me in my apartment and all I can think about is having sex with him again. I'm going to kill Becca the next time I see her.

I search for reasons why we can't continue that kiss, and nothing else exists but the hungry way he's looking at me, the worried emotion in his dark gaze.

Pressing closer, I crash my mouth against his again. He makes a noise of surprise in the back of his throat, but it only takes a moment before he brings both hands to my jaw, kissing me deeply, his tongue reaching out to stroke mine.

Then his lips still, and he pulls back just a fraction. "E, you're drunk."

I shake my head. "Not that drunk."

He kisses me again, his tongue eagerly tangling with mine. *His kisses are sooo good.* I've never been kissed like this. So deep and demanding and hard. He kisses like he plays hockey—with complete confidence and laser focus.

"Are you pissed at me?" he asks between kisses.

"Yes." I pull his lips back to mine with one hand around the back of his neck. But that doesn't mean I'm ready to stop kissing him. *God, there's just something about this man.*

"No one can ever know." His voice is husky and a little desperate, and damn if that doesn't light me up like the fourth of July, my nipples hardening in my bra and my stomach squeezing with lust.

I nod, closing my fist in the front of his sweatshirt. "Agreed. Especially not my brother." I pull back suddenly, needing space between us. Needing to see his eyes. He looks down at me in wonder, his lips damp and swollen from my kisses. "But don't ghost on me again. We're friends right?"

He touches my cheek with his thumb. "Yeah. And I really am sorry about that. I won't ghost on you ever again. It's been the longest few months of my life watching you and not knowing how to repair this. I can't go through that again."

Using my grip on his shirt, I tug him closer and we fall back onto the couch together, me on my back with him on top of me. He balances his weight on his forearms as he hovers over me, caging me in with his massive biceps and firm hips. There is nowhere I'd rather be in this moment. Which is crazy right? I should be mad at him. And maybe I am a little, but I've spent months agonizing over that night. Now the only thing that makes sense is erasing that memory with a better one.

"This isn't smart," I say to myself as much as to him.

"Turns out I get kind of stupid around you," he says, voice brimming with emotion.

His mouth is on my throat, his tongue tracing circles along my racing pulse, and I frantically push my hips closer to his, my body clenching down wildly when I feel the firm ridge in his jeans. I press myself closer, grinding myself right up against it.

He lets out a soft groan. "Fuck."

His mouth covers mine again, his kisses growing more desperate.

It's such a turn on.

My phone starts ringing from its spot on the coffee table, not even two feet away.

I let out a frustrated sigh and grab it to look at the display. It's probably just Becca being nosy. But nope. *Shit.*

"It's my brother," I announce.

Justin's lips leave my neck and his cock immediately stops grinding against my core. I miss the feel of him instantly.

Damn it. I've been cock-blocked by my own brother.

"You better answer that or he'll get suspicious."

I nod. "Hey." My voice comes out shakier than I expected.

"Hey. You didn't text me when you got home."

I swallow. "Yeah, sorry, I forgot. I'm home. Everything's good."

"Cool," Owen says. "Brady's still not back yet."

I press one hand against Justin's chest and he rises up off of me, sitting beside me and watching me with a worried expression.

"Oh, well he mentioned something about stopping for food."

"Gotcha. Okay, well I'll see you soon, right?"

"Yep. Love you."

As soon as I hang up, I bite my lip and stand. "You better go."

"Yeah, I know." He pulls me up from the couch and while we're standing, he has to lean down and lower his mouth to mine to kiss me. I wrap my arms around his bulky shoulders and lean into him, savoring the contact.

"Night, Justin."

"Goodnight, Elise" he says, his deep voice is raspy, and I revel in the idea that maybe, just maybe I affect him as much as he does me.

CHAPTER ELEVEN

Black Eyes and Blue Balls

Justin

Now that the season has officially started back up, we're on night one of a four-day trip to the northeast. We'll have a game in Boston tomorrow night and then one in New York before we head back home. Back-to-back roadies usually require all my mental focus, but instead all I can think about is that kiss Elise and I shared the night I drove her home.

After landing in Boston, we went to the rink for a warm-up and had a team dinner at a nice steakhouse. Now it's not even nine and I'm in my hotel room. Owen and I always share an adjoining room, and the doors between our rooms stay open unless one of us is entertaining for the evening.

He's sitting in the armchair near the windows playing on his phone while I lay sprawled across the bed.

I can tell based on the spark in his eyes and the easy grin on his face that he's making plans for later.

"What's her name?" I ask.

Owen laughs. "Not sure yet. I'm on Tinder scoping out my options." He taps out some response on the screen, looking pleased. "You're coming out later, right?"

"No. I'm fucking exhausted man."

"Pussy," he mutters under his breath.

I shake my head. Owen's just built different. The pressures of the game never seem to affect him. He's as cool, calm and collected right before a playoff game as he is when we're down by three in the third period. Nothing shakes the dude.

It's probably that attitude that got him called up the pros. While I was drafted straight into the league at barely nineteen and made the pro roster right away, Owen spent two years playing in the minors, proving himself worthy. He wasn't worried even then. It's one of the things I appreciate most about the guy, and it makes him an amazing goalie. He's got nerves of steel.

And despite that, he's always got a ready grin, and he's always down for mischief. Which used to be something we had in common, but lately something's changed inside me. But it doesn't matter, because all of my available focus needs to be on winning games. Especially since half of my brain seems to be stuck on a girl I have no right to be thinking about.

Owen lets out a long sigh and stretches his arms overhead. "Honestly, I'm tired too, I just want to decompress for a little while, have a beer, and maybe have a little fun." He waggles his eyebrows.

"Good luck with that," I chuckle, shaking my head.

"I don't need luck with this moneymaker." He points to his face and smiles.

Ignoring him, I grab my phone from the duvet cover beside me and see a text from Elise.

Good luck tomorrow.

It feels somehow wrong, almost naughty to text her back while her brother is in my room. But he's busy on his phone too. What could it hurt?

What are you doing right now?

Three dots appear that tell me she's replying—
and I'm smiling. Why am I smiling?

"Hey I'm going to head out. You cool?" Owen
stands, pocketing his phone.

"Yeah, I'm good. Good night, man."

He disappears into his own room, and closes
the door behind him, and I glance down to see
Elise's reply.

Just got home from work a little
while ago.

I forgot it's a few hours earlier there.

You guys going out tonight?

I smirk to myself. She knows our routine well
I suppose.

No, I'm staying in.

```
Why aren't you going out with
the guys?
```

Her text feels like she's baiting me, but I'm not scared to tell her the truth. There have been too many secrets between us for too long now.

```
Because I'm thinking about some-
                        one else.
```

```
Oh really? I wonder who the lucky
lady is.;)
```

I chuckle to myself, enjoying this flirty side of Elise. I type:

```
I want to continue that kiss.
```

She responds: `When are you back?`

Straight to the point. I like it. Grinning, I reply:

```
                    Not until Sunday.
```

It's Wednesday now and suddenly that feels

like forever away. Stupid east coast games.

Okay we can hang out then if you want.

Sounds perfect to me.

Goodnight then. She writes.

Noooo. Don't go yet.

What are you wearing?

There's a long pause and I wonder if I pushed too hard too fast. Then her message pops up:

Nice try. Go get some sleep. And win tomorrow's game for me?

Done, I reply.

I fall asleep that night with thoughts of Elise and a smile on my face. Maybe, just maybe, I can make amends for my fucked-up behavior before.

It's doubtful, but if I can make Elise smile, I'll try anything.

• • •

The entire mood on the bench changes in the split-second it takes for the puck to slide into the net, despite Owen's best efforts. We're down by two goals in the first period, which is a shit way to start our first away game. We've only been playing ten freaking minutes.

And even though he's given up two, somehow Owen's not even rattled. I can see him grinning from behind his face mask across the ice. *Cocky motherfucker.*

Coach Bryant adjusts his tie, looking uncomfortable and frankly a little pissed off as he paces behind the bench.

I grab one of the water bottles in front of me and squirt some in my mouth, chest heaving. I desperately need to keep my focus. There's no way in fuck I'm losing to Boston in game one. That is not happening.

"Let's fucking go!" Grant, our team captain, yells as our line jumps the wall to take the ice again.

In the end—we squeak by with a win. The highlights? I skated my ass off, ended up scoring two goals, was hip-checked into the boards hard enough to bruise my ribs, but it's all good because we won.

The New York game goes a little better. We dominate the first two periods, but then in the third, I get into a fight that leaves me with a bruised eye that's quickly swelling.

But as we board the plane home, the only thing I care about is the fact we are now two for two. My ribs are bruised and I'm probably on my way to having a black eye, but injuries like these are fairly common after games. It's nothing a little rest and ice won't fix.

I settle into my seat, and put my headphones on. I'm not in the mood to listen to music right now, I just don't want to hear the trash-talking from the card game happening in the row behind me.

Our trainer Sven comes over and takes the seat next to me. "How's the eye feel?"

I shrug, removing my headphones. "I've had worse. It'll be fine."

He's incredibly fit for an old dude and highly respected by the entire team. He's worked for the league for more than twenty-five years. When Sven tells you to do something, you do it. And right now he's frowning at me. "The team doctor is worried about a concussion. You have an appointment to go see him in the morning."

Well shit.

"Fine. I'll be there."

Sven nods and gets up to return to his seat near the front of the plane.

I put the headphones back on, and pull my phone out of my pocket to see a text from Elise.

```
Are you okay? I watched the game
on TV. That fight looked brutal.
```

```
I'm okay but we might need to
take a raincheck. The only thing
I'm in the mood for is a hot
shower, a pain pill and my bed.
```

Her reply comes in a second later.

```
No problem. Feel better.
```

I'm a tiny bit worried about that concussion

comment from Sven, but I don't want to scare Elise. I'm more worried that I won't get to play next weekend, but I don't want her to worry too, so I don't say anything. The other reason I don't want to show up at her place tonight is because I'm pretty sure by the time we land, my eye will have gone from bruised and tender to purple and swollen shut.

CHAPTER TWELVE

Goals

Elise

"**W**hat about this one?" I hold up a plum-colored silk sheath dress for Becca to inspect.

She narrows her eyes. "That depends on what your goals are for tonight."

I chuckle. "My goals?" We're inside a trendy boutique downtown and I've already talked myself into splurging.

Becca rounds the rack of cocktail dresses and begins searching through the hangers on the other side. "Yes. Since you're so dead set on this. Let's talk about your goals."

I'd told Becca about the kiss Justin and I shared. Well, it was more than just a kiss. Remembering the way his hard body caged mine in against my couch while we grinded together has inspired new fantasies every night for the past week. Which is unfortunately almost as long as it's been since I've seen him. We've both had busy weeks, and we can't exactly parade this little fling in front of my brother. Which has meant we haven't gotten any time to explore that kiss further, but I plan on changing that tonight.

Justin invited me to a charity banquet the team is attending tonight. Becca's required to be there too, but she's had her dress picked out forever— a strapless black thing she always wears to these events—her words, not mine.

As far as Owen knows, Justin invited me as a friend so I can hang out with Becca and drink free champagne.

"My *goal*," I say, shoving the plum colored sheath back onto the rack, "is to have fun. I've never had a fling before."

Becca makes a noise of disagreement. For the record, she thinks this is a terrible idea. "That's the thing though. It can't be purely physical when you have major feels for the person."

I roll my eyes. "I don't have major feels." *I*

don't think. Do I?

She narrows her eyes at me, her full lips pressing into a line dramatically.

"Okay, I did. At one time, yes. But then," I pause, gauging our surroundings. I can't actually say that he punched my v-card in the quiet boutique with the owner hovering nearby. I straighten my posture and lower my voice. "After all that *stuff* that went down between us, I accepted that he's not capable of more. He doesn't do feelings and romance, and that's fine. That's not what I'm looking for at this stage in my life."

Becca looks skeptical, but she doesn't say anything else, weighing my words.

But I keep talking. "We have chemistry, we always have. And if I can have a little fun with that, then why the heck not?"

"Why not? Um, because it's a terrible fucking idea, that's why not," Becca scoffs.

She abandons the rack we've been searching and heads to the other side of the store. I follow her, already eyeing an emerald colored dress I spot from across the room. *I wonder if I can pull off emerald?*

I pull a deep breath into my lungs and inspect the emerald dress—that beading on the neckline is way too much. Then I turn to her, trying to find the words that will make her understand what's going on in my head, my heart. "Becca, you of all people have always been all sex-positive, female-friendly, feminist super power go rah, rah love."

Her eyebrows dart up. And then she bursts out laughing. "Rah, rah love? Seriously?"

"Yeah, sorry. That was probably a little much," I laugh. "But seriously Becca, think about it. Why can't I fuck around and have fun? The guys do it all the time." *Understatement of the year.* My brother and his friends make an Olympic sport out of no-strings sex, and they are all gold-medalists—many times over. I thrust my shoulders back. "And if anyone needs a redo, it's me and Justin." That part was true at least. I needed to erase the memories of that night and replace them with something sweeter. It's more than a desire, it's practically a necessity. *I need this.* I need to be the one in control this time. And I need Becca to see that.

Becca thinks it over for a moment, then heaves out a long sigh. "Fine."

"Fine?" That's it? She's agreeing with me now? What in the ever-loving fuck? We've been debating this for almost three days now.

She shrugs. "You're right, okay? If you can keep yourself objective about this—if you can promise me that you won't get emotionally attached—that you won't…"

I hold up one hand. "I promise you, I'm in it for the orgasms. That's it."

Becca finally breaks into a smile. "Girl, he better deliver or I'm going to tell Owen and we're both going to kick his ass."

I raise my brows. "You would never tell Owen. Would you?" My brother would not do well knowing that Justin and I had boned. There would be blood, and tears and yeah, it would *not* be good.

"Of course not," Becca continues, eyes narrowed on a red dress. "But I will kick Justin's ass if he does even *one* freaking thing to upset you. And I mean that. He's all out of free passes. He's got one shot at this, and the second he pisses you off, that's it as far as I'm concerned."

Her expression is as serious as a heart attack. God, I love her. "Deal." I nod. I like that plan— he's got one shot and the minute it turns not fun, I'm out.

Becca, grinning like she's won this debate, nods once to me before turning to peruse a rack of dresses. Even though she's a pain in the ass, I love her, and I'm thankful for our friendship, and her sage advice.

"Oh my God. This is it," Becca says, holding up a hanger for me to see. There's a pale-pink lace shift dress with a deep V-neck in the front and back dangling delicately from the hanger. It's so pretty. It's innocent, but also sexy. It's me.

It's also four hundred dollars, but I told myself I was going to splurge.

"It's perfect. I'll take it."

CHAPTER THIRTEEN

Playing the Game

Elise

Everyone's here tonight. Owen, the entire team, Coach Bryant, several players I don't recognize out of their gear, Becca, me, and most distracting of all—Justin.

He's dressed in a finely tailored black tuxedo, crisp white shirt and enough sex appeal to thaw an entire ice rink in three seconds flat.

We'd ridden together in a limo over to the event. I sat between Becca and Owen, but with Justin seated across from us in the dimly lit interior, my mind had immediately scrambled in sixteen different directions and my heart beat so hard I was scared everyone in the limo could hear it. It had taken some serious level of Jedi strength to force myself to not stare at him the entire ride, and based on the way his eyes smoldered, he appreciated my dress.

Once inside the huge ballroom, we made the rounds, mingling and exchanging hellos. I quickly had two glasses of champagne and then accepted Justin's offer to dance.

I've never danced with him before, but the seven-piece jazz band is inspiring, and he's a much better dancer than I would have imagined. Maybe playing hockey all those years has made him light on his feet, who knows.

He places his hands innocently against my waist while I rest mine against the lapels of his jacket. It's been ten days since we made out and there's an urgent sexual attraction buzzing between us, but we're supposed to be acting like we're just friends, so dancing is as far as it's going to get.

There's a faint dark bruise beneath his left eye, and I have the strangest impulse to kiss him there. My lips twitch with that secret knowledge.

"What is it?" he asks, amused by me.

I shake my head. He's way too perceptive. "Nothing. It's not important."

"Tell me." His voice is steady, and sure when I

feel anything but.

"I just had this strange reaction—I wanted to kiss your black eye and make it feel better."

His gaze locks onto mine, his blue eyes dark and filled with emotion as he watches me. "My eye feels fine, but I could think of a few other places that I'd like your kisses."

I raise one eyebrow at him. "Is that so?"

He shakes his head, chuckling. "You're going to get me in trouble."

I meet his eyes. "How would I get you in trouble?"

He pulls me closer, under the guise of dancing. "Because when I suddenly get an erection while dancing with you, Owen is going to beat my ass. And I've been in more fights on the ice than I can remember, but I've never gotten into a brawl wearing a tuxedo."

I can't help the laugh that tumbles from my lips.

His eyebrows dart up. "You think that's funny, huh?"

He presses his hips closer, and the laughter dies on my lips. In fact, all the breath leaves my lungs at once. Because holy shit. He wasn't kidding about being hard. There's a steely rod pressing behind his zipper, and all we've done is dance—at a safe enough distance to make any middle-school chaperone happy.

I grin up at him, feeling a little cheeky. "Hey there, big boy."

He chuckles darkly, gaze hot. "Don't."

"Is that a hockey stick, or are you just happy to see me?" I tease.

"Elise," he warns, voice now tight.

I've never felt quite so powerful, quite so desirable. He wants me. This sexy, god of a man wants *me*. The feeling is quickly becoming addictive.

His fingers slide along the exposed skin on my back, settling low and resting just above my ass. Just as I'm contemplating asking him how soon we can get out of here, my attention is captured by Owen approaching us. Justin moves his hand to a more innocent spot against the middle of my back and separates our bodies with a couple of extra inches. I hate it immediately.

But I smile at my brother. "Hey, Owen."

"Hey." He looks directly at Justin, eyes narrowing. "I'm going to get out of here. You'll take care of Elise?"

"Of course," Justin says without hesitation.

And just like that, I'm immediately picturing all the ways Justin Brady can *take care of me* tonight. Most of them are while I'm naked and horizontal, but Owen doesn't need to know that.

Owen gives Justin a solemn look, nods once, and then returns to his date, placing his hand against the small of her back as he ushers her to the exit.

I've never seen the girl he's with before, but I don't bother asking her name, because I'm also certain I'll never see her again. *My brother the manwhore, ladies and gentlemen.*

Justin and I finish our dance and go to the bar to get another drink.

Predictably, Asher and Teddy disappear halfway through the evening with their dates, because heaven forbid they go one night without getting some action.

Actually, Justin is the same way. Becca's right about that. But this time I'm okay with it because for once we're on the same page. This is just for pleasure, nothing serious.

Just after the coach finally leaves, Becca comes to find me.

"I'm going to go. Are you guys staying?" She looks meaningfully between me and Justin.

He pulls my hand into his lap. It's a bold move, but almost everyone else is gone. "I'll make sure she gets home safely. Goodnight, Becca."

Is it just me, or is it kind of hot how he just dismissed her?

She gives me a playful wink. "Okay then. It's sounds like you two kids have this under control."

Justin leans close to my ear, biting his lip. "She knows, doesn't she?"

My stomach fills with nerves. This is supposed to be a secret between us, I know that. But surely he doesn't expect me to withhold this from my best friend? Plus, I don't think Justin will be mad that I told Becca. First, Becca is trustworthy. Second, Justin has never gotten mad at me once in my entire life. And I was a very bratty, hormonal pre-teen. "I needed some advice. So, yeah. I talked to her."

He nods, looking down at me. "It's fine. I just want us to be careful. This is just for fun, right? No feelings. No one gets hurt. Two friends enjoying each other's company."

I nod quickly. "Exactly."

"You ready to get out of here?"

I lick my lips. I fight the urge to say something cheesy like, *I thought you'd never ask*, and instead opt for a brief *sure*.

Actually, it comes out as more a squeak, but Justin doesn't seem to mind.

He grins, pleased with me and leads the way to the exit.

Fucking finally. My ovaries do a happy dance as we climb into a car for the ride home. I'm not sure what happened to the limo—if it took others home or was just a one-way thing, but it doesn't matter. Sitting in the back of a car alone with Justin feels incredibly intimate and I like the closeness.

It smells like leather and him, and *oh my God*, I can't believe this is real.

His hand rests on my knee as the driver pulls the car into traffic. When I give the driver my address, he tells me the bridge is out and traffic is at a standstill.

"My place is five minutes away, let's go there,"

says Justin.

"What about Owen?" I ask.

He looks at me with a puzzled expression. "He won't be home tonight. He never brings bunnies back to our place if he can help it."

My shoulders tense for just a second. But then I realize he's right. Owen's quirk of not taking a hookup to his bed isn't exactly a state secret. It's weird, and gross, but Justin's right.

"Plus, he'd never come in my room if my door was shut."

I nod, still feeling a little unsure as Justin rattles off the address.

He glances at me. "If you're really worried about it, my bedroom door has a lock."

I take a deep breath, visibly relaxing. He's right. It'll be fine. Worst case scenario, we could say I was too drunk to go home and was just there to crash on the couch.

When the driver pulls to stop in front of Justin and Owen's building, we climb out and head inside. And I find that Justin was right. It's dark and quiet inside. But it still feels incredibly strange to be here at my brother's apartment sneaking around.

I make sure to take my purse and my heels and I immediately head into Justin's bedroom. He follows me, smirking.

"You okay?"

I nod. "A little nervous, but yeah."

"What can I do?" he asks, moving closer and placing his hands on my bare upper arms. His touch grounds me and I immediately feel more calm.

"Will you bring me a glass of water?"

"Of course." He leaves and returns a second later with a tall glass of ice water.

I take a long drink and then place it on the table beside the bed with shaking hands while Justin closes the door to his room. He turns on the lamp in the corner, creating the perfect amount of ambient lighting and then turns on some soft music from his laptop. I notice the playlist is called Chill Vibes on Spotify. It's melodic and calm. I make a mental note to check it out later. But then he comes back to where I'm standing and the moment changes. It's filled with expectation and meaning.

Suddenly I realize I have no fucking idea what I'm doing here or how this is supposed to go, and I'm immediately self-conscious. The one and only time I've had sex was with him, and alcohol was involved. Now we both know what we're here to do and I'm more nervous this time.

He looks so sexy standing in front of me in his tux. He lifts both my hands and places them against his waist. Then he puts his hands on my hips, gripping me lightly.

"You look a little anxious. Are you sure you're okay?"

I nod. "Yeah. I mean, I am nervous. But I'm okay."

"Tell me what I can do to help." His voice is low and sensual and chill bumps race along my exposed arms.

"I guess I'm just remembering the last time I was in this room with you."

Releasing his hold on me, he scrubs one hand through his hair, messing up the neat style, and hefts out a sigh. "Yeah, I kind of fucked that up, didn't I?"

My mouth lifts in a half-grin. "A little bit."

"Can I ask you something?" He suddenly looks unsure.

I nod.

"That night … were you a virgin?" His deep blue gaze is locked on mine, and my chest suddenly feels tight.

I figured he'd been too drunk to notice. Hell, I wasn't even sure he knew it was *me* in his bed. And yet, I'd wanted him anyway.

I lick my lower lip. "Yeah."

His expression turns pained and his eyebrows push together. "Why didn't you tell me?"

I realize my hands are still resting on his waist where he placed them. He touches my cheek, lifting my chin toward his so I'm forced to meet his eyes. But the sweet concern in them is more than I can take and I blink and look away.

"I'm not sure," I say. And I'm really not. I never found the right moment to press the pause button and say oh by the way, I've never done this before, but I always dreamed you'd be my first.

"I could have made it better for you. I could have been more careful." He's still touching my cheek, his fingers splayed along my jaw.

I look up and meet his eyes again. "We need a do-over," I murmur as his mouth slowly descends on mine.

He kisses me softly once before pulling back. "I think I could help with that."

I smile up at him, and lift on my toes to press my lips to his once more. They're soft and pliable and he smells so good.

I'm glad he doesn't press the issue further. I'm really glad he doesn't ask why I wanted to share my first time with him, because I'm afraid I'll admit the extent of my feelings, and since I've vowed to turn them off, it's not a piece of information I can divulge. Those days are done and behind me, I just want to forget about it and have a hot fling with a hot man. I've assured Becca it's possible, and I hate being wrong.

"You looked so sexy tonight. I didn't get to tell you that before." He releases his touch on my cheek and shrugs out of his jacket. He tosses it on the chair in the corner, and then he's pulling at the silk bow tie to unknot it while his gaze stays glued to mine.

I finally reach up and run my thumb carefully along the faint bruise underneath his eye. His lips part, but he stays completely still, letting me explore. His stubble is rough against my palm as my hand slides down his cheek. Then I draw him closer, urging his lips back to mine.

This seems to spark something in him and his kiss turns molten hot—his tongue seeking entrance and tangling with mine. I make a low, desperate sound in my throat, and suddenly Justin's fingers are at the nape of my neck. He draws the zipper of my dress down my spine with a satisfying low hiss.

I don't break our kiss to slide the dress off my shoulders, or even when it falls to the floor in a puddle around my bare feet.

And I'm still sucking on his tongue, still making needy sounds when his hands descend on my curves, caressing over my ribs down to my hips, until I feel his calloused palms gripping my ass—which he uses to haul me closer.

He lets out a soft grunt when my pelvis rubs against the impressive bulge in his pants, and a warm shudder pulses through me at the contact. His hands stay on my ass, kneading the flesh of my cheeks while my trembling fingers move to the front of his dress shirt to begin working on the buttons.

He pulls the shirttails from his pants, and then shrugs it off, dropping it to the floor. A half-naked man in front of me would be an exciting thing. A half-naked pro athlete ratchets everything up to a whole other level. His chiseled muscles and smooth, tanned skin are perfection. His pec muscles and abs are downright lickable, and those biceps would have no problem supporting my weight while he fucked me. The nude-colored lace thong I'm wearing instantly grows damp at that thought.

His body is built for sin and whatever qualms I had about tonight vanish in an instant. I want this. I want him. I damn well deserve it.

I reach for his belt and begin tugging it free.

His lips break from mine and he gazes at me in wonder. One hand is still on my ass, and the other is now buried in the hair at the back of my neck. "Are you sure about this?" he asks, voice thick.

I realize this is it. He's giving me a moment to consider if I want to back out. A second to contemplate what a 'friends with benefits' arrangement could mean if my brother ever found out. And I know he wouldn't hold it against me if I chose to hit the brakes on this entire thing.

It's sweet of him, but I shake my head. "I want this." I pause, weighing my words, in an attempt to clear my head. I *need* to be the one in control here—it has to be me calling the shots or this will never work. "As long as we both agree this stays casual—no feelings, no one gets hurt."

Justin doesn't say anything for a moment as he processes this, but I see an unmistakable flash of understanding behind his eyes. "You're right. We can't have anything ruin our friendship, or complicate things with your brother."

"Exactly." I nod. "The second one of us starts to develop real feelings, we have to communicate immediately, and then the fun stops."

Owen is not just Justin's best friend, but also his roommate, and a teammate, and they have a demanding job and a schedule that can't allow either of them to lose focus and fuck up their careers. It seems like we're on the same page with this. It's just a fling. Nothing more. Nothing less.

"Okay," he says. And then his lips are back on mine and he gives me a playful shove. I fall onto his bed, resting on my elbows as I watch him stand in front of me. He tugs the belt free and drops it onto the floor. And then he reaches one hand inside his pants to adjust his stiff length and I almost groan.

He lowers himself to his knees on the side of

the bed, grabs onto my ankles, and pulls me until my butt is close to the edge of the mattress. Planting his mouth on my inner thigh, he leaves wet, sucking kisses as he moves lower, until he's nuzzling me, softly biting me, right over the lace of my panties.

I let out a moan of frustration and thread my fingers into his dark, silky hair. Tonight could not be going any better, even if I'd scripted it. *Eat your heart out, Becca.*

CHAPTER FOURTEEN

All You Can Eat Buffet

Justin

God I could eat her all night. Elise squirms on my bed, her pale curves so beautiful against my bedding. I plant chaste kisses along the lace of her panties and appreciate the way she whimpers and thrusts her hands into my hair.

After one last open-mouthed kiss right over her center, I peel her damp panties away, tugging until she lifts her ass and I can remove them completely. Her natural instinct is to close her knees, but I shake my head.

"Don't hide this perfect pussy from me." My voice comes out so deep and husky, but I don't bother clearing my throat because I doubt it will help. I'm so fucking turned on right now, my dick is leaking pre-come in my boxer briefs and she hasn't even touched me yet.

She groans and throws her forearm over her eyes. "Oh God. You don't have to…"

"Have to what?" I grin up at her, amused by her shy reaction. "Eat your pussy?"

She nods, cheeks slightly pink.

"Trust me, baby, I do. I've been dreaming of this moment for way too long."

She lets out a squeak of surprise that turns into a moan the second my tongue touches her sweet flesh.

"Oh my fuck," she gasps, gripping the back of my neck with one trembling hand.

"That's it," I murmur, tongue lapping against her in a slow, steady rhythm. "Let me make this pretty little pussy come." I bite her inner thigh and give her perfect cunt a light slap. "Would that be okay with you?"

"Oh fuck," Elise moans, shivering from the pleasure when I return my mouth to its rightful place and take a long, deep suck of her clit.

If I weren't so incredibly turned on right now, I could almost chuckle at her responses. She's so primal and needy, grinding against my face, pressing my head closer with her hands, and pushing her hips off the bed to get my mouth closer—which I am not opposed to—trust me. I love how into this she is, and I really love that it's *me* causing these reactions from her.

I reach into my pants and give the base of my cock a warning squeeze. I'm so heavy and hard, I need to calm myself the fuck down before I embarrass myself. It's like my dick knows how good the sex is going to be and it's eager to blow this for me. Actually the word *blow* is not helping matters. The visual of Elise on her knees before me, those pouty lips taking my cock is too hot for words.

I make a sound that's half grunt, half frustrated need and lightly bite her clit.

Her hips shoot off the bed. "Did you just *bite* me?"

I look up at her and grin. "Yes."

"Ohhh." Her eyes sink closed in pleasure and she moans long and low in her throat.

I give her another gentle nibble before adding one finger, pushing my middle finger slowly inside her hot, tight heat.

I groan again when I feel how warm and wet she is and my cock jerks behind my zipper.

"Oh God." She shudders.

I take my time, licking and sucking her in time to the steady movement of my finger. I could do this all fucking night. I made a lot of mistakes the first time we were together. I don't intend to make any tonight. In fact, I vow to make it my mission to see to it that she has as many orgasms as she can handle.

I increase my tempo and Elise pants.

"Yes. Like that. Fuck." Her voice is hoarse and so sexy. "Just like that."

Her muscles tighten and I sense how close she is. I don't let up, not even when she curses my name and her tight body clenches around my finger.

Letting her ride the high of her orgasm for as long as possible—until her body twitches with overstimulation—I finally withdraw my finger and plant an open-mouthed kiss on her inner thigh.

"That feel good, baby?"

"That was …" She pants and lifts up on her elbows, mouth lifting in a satisfied smile. "Get up here."

I'm grinning as I make my way up over her body and onto the bed. I pull her warm, pliable body into my arms and Elise sighs.

My lips slant over hers at the exact moment we both hear it. The slamming of the front door and heavy, uncoordinated footsteps falling over the wood floors. My heart stutters for a moment and my stomach tightens.

"Brady!" Owen calls from the hall. "You in there?"

Oh fuck.

My erection is pressed right up against her wet pussy.

I swallow down a wave of nerves, fighting to compose myself so I don't sound like I'm about to blow my load. "Yeah. I'm a little busy at the moment. Talk later?"

He laughs. "Sorry to interrupt."

Elise's eyes, wide with panic are latched onto mine. "Oh my God!" she whispers, clamping one hand over her lips.

"Shh. It's okay." Meeting her eyes, I smooth one hand over her hair. I hope my voice is more convincing than I sound, because there's no denying how fucked up this is. My tongue still tastes like Elise's delicious pussy and her brother is standing on the other side of my door. My unlocked bedroom door.

"Do you want to keep going?" I ask. "I can lock the door."

She shakes her head. "How am I going to get out of here?" she whispers.

I press my lips to hers. "It'll be okay."

Somehow.

I fucking hope.

With superhuman strength, I leave the warmth of her on my bed and stand. I have to adjust myself again, tucking my cock beneath the waistband of my pants because there's no way my erection is going to fade after what I just experienced.

Fuck, I don't know how I'll ever not be hard again.

Elise's gaze tracking my every movement is not helping matters. There's still a want in her eyes that's hard to ignore.

"Stay here," I whisper.

She shakes her head eyes still wide with worry.

I press a kiss to her forehead. "Stay here. It'll be okay. Lock the door behind me if you want."

Understanding registers in her eyes. I'm going to try my best to get rid of him, but if he's intoxicated, I'm not quite sure how this is going to go.

I shrug on a t-shirt from my closet as Elise quickly puts her panties and dress back on. I'm actually pissed off about the fact that her bra never came off, but I thought we had all night. Vowing to rectify that next time, I swallow my anger and exit the room, heading out into the hall.

Owen's sitting on the couch, the remote in his hand, some sports highlights show on the TV.

"Hey, dude."

His head turns toward mine. "Hey." Then his eyebrows wiggle. "You busy fucking?"

I force myself to laugh, but I actually feel more like throwing up. That's his baby *fucking* sister in there. I can still feel the way she clenched around my finger and moaned my name when she came. I am a grade A asshole.

My stomach tightens as I sit down next to him on the couch. Owen keeps talking but I don't hear a damn word he says. Blood thunders in my ears and guilt swarms inside me.

"You have someone in there?" he finally says, turning toward me with a confused expression.

"No." I deny it too quickly and I'm sure he's suspicious.

"I heard … sounds." He grins.

"Oh yeah." I thrust one hand through my hair. "I was watching porn."

The lie tastes bitter on my tongue, but what the fuck else can I say?

Owen laughs. "Right on, dude. I struck out tonight too."

I'm a little surprised, considering he left with a woman, but I don't press him.

"Then let's go get out of here, let's go get one more beer. My treat." I rise to my feet, hoping like hell he takes the bait.

After a moment's hesitation, he shrugs. "Why the fuck not."

It's not the most genius plan in the world, but I need to get Owen out of the apartment so Elise can sneak out. It's the only thing I can think of when I still having a raging, and rather neglected, erection between my thighs.

After Owen and I exit the apartment, I shoot off a text to Elise.

> I am so fucking sorry. I didn't think he'd come home tonight.

She replies after a few seconds.

> Did you guys just leave?

Owen's busy on his phone, and so I don't hesitate I snap a quick reply back to her.

> Yes, I thought it best to get him out of the apartment so you could leave. Again, I'm so fucking sorry.

Her reply is just a laughing face emoji.

I release a slow exhale, thankful she's not pissed off. I just asked her to sneak out of my apartment rather than deal with the situation like a man. It's not my best moment.

> Oh my God thank you. You're a

genius. I'm leaving now.

I don't feel like a genius, I feel like an asshole. An asshole who needs to blow my load. We exit the elevator and then leave our building, walking toward the little dive bar that's closest to our place. Tonight feels like the punchline to a bad joke. I've waited three months for this and all I get is the taste of her perfect pussy on my lips and the world's worst case of blue balls. My fingers are busy typing out another apology to Elise.

I feel awful. How mad are you right now?

Her reply comes in just as we reach the front door to the bar. I pull it open and wait for Owen to step through. While he leads the way to the bar, I look down to read her response.

Not mad. I feel bad about leaving you like THAT.

I get the sense that THAT is code for the monster erection that's still aching in my pants.

I force my thumbs into action.

                              I'll live.

I didn't get to return the favor.

    : (

God, this girl. She's fucking killing me.

            I probably deserved it.

Owen and I reach the bar, and we take a seat on
two barstools. The place is mostly deserted tonight.
I take a brief glance down to see Elise's reply.

I guess it's karma for you ghost-
ing before.

I shake my head and chuckle, then type:

                           Exactly.

"Who are you texting with? You're so distracted," Owens asks, eyes narrowing.

"No one. Sorry." I shove my phone into my

pocket so I'm not tempted to look at it again.

"This guy's paying," he announces to the bartender with a smirk, then he orders the most expensive whiskey on the menu. Thirty bucks a glass.

I reach for my back pocket and shake my head. *Shit.*

"I forgot my wallet," I croak.

Owen rolls his eyes. "Fucker."

In my haste to get out of the apartment, I'm dressed in a pair of tuxedo pants, a Nirvana t-shirt, and my Vans with no socks. And apparently no wallet. It's quite an ensemble.

I order a beer on Owen and promise to pay him back, but he just shakes his head. He makes millions of dollars a year. He doesn't need me to buy him a drink anyway.

As I listen to him give a recap on his night, I find myself drifting away to memories of my own night. Memories of how stunning Elise looked in that little pink dress, of how good she felt in my arms. I'm desperate to pull my phone out and check for more messages from her, but I don't dare do it yet.

Finally, Owen excuses himself to the bathroom, and I fumble for my phone, fucking up the passcode three times in my haste to unlock it.

I quickly type out a message and hit send.

```
Just wanted to make sure you got
                    home safe.
```

Her reply is quick: `I'm home now. Thank you for tonight.`

```
Thank you for sharing your gor-
   geous body with me,
```
I type back.

It's a little cheesy, but fuck it. I click send just as Owen comes strolling back from the restroom. He sits down beside me and takes a sip of his whiskey.

As I slip my phone back in my pocket, he turns to me and slaps a hand on my shoulder.

"Thanks for bringing Elise tonight so she could hang out with Becca. I know she's been down since that guy dumped her."

Guilt churns low in my stomach. "It was nothing," I choke out the words and take a long drink of the beer that's been placed in front of me.

He shakes his head and gives me a slight smile. "You're a good friend."

He wouldn't be saying that to me if he knew that I still have the taste of her on my tongue, and that my dick is aching to be inside of her as we speak.

I feel like a huge, lying asshole, and I hate how my choices are either to hurt Elise or to lie to Owen. There's just no gray area, only black and white about this situation, and it sucks.

Rock meet hard place.

CHAPTER FIFTEEN

Can't Hold Us Down

Elise

I'm used to the constant feeling of needing to throw up while watching a hockey game. That's nothing new. My brother, the team's star goalie, has always been calm under the pressure, but I joke with him that's only because I'm nervous enough for the both of us. Still, I wouldn't miss this game for all the money in the world—queasy stomach aside.

My chest tightens as I lean forward in my third row seat, watching the action on the ice unfold. The guys have only been playing for a couple of minutes now, and as nice as it is watching Owen play, my eyes are on someone else tonight.

Justin Brady. Number thirty-six. And my own

personal walking, and skating, fantasy come to life. *God, he's perfection.*

He and I both had a busy week, and haven't spent any time alone together since I snuck out of his apartment in the middle of the night after the banquet, but that doesn't mean he's been far from my thoughts. I've been able to think of little else. We've also texted every night. And the last few nights, our texting has been kicking up a notch, turning naughty and sexy.

Our nightly messages are something I now look forward to. He's funny. And sweet. But of course, I'm still on guard. I know with certainty that I can't fall for him. This is just for fun. As long as I remember that, I'll be fine.

Watching him skate and move almost defies logic. He's so quick and agile, but so aggressive at the same time. It's kind of a turn on if I'm being honest. His broad shoulders twist as he angles his body away from the opposing player charging at him, managing to stay upright in the process.

"You want anything?" Becca asks from beside me. "I'm going to get some food from the concessions. I'm starving."

I shake my head, eyes still out on the action.

"I'll wait until intermission." There's no way I want to miss a single moment of this game.

She chuckles at me as she rises to her feet. "I'll bring you back a pretzel."

Eyes still on the ice, I grin. She knows me well. "Perfect." The number of times I've eaten a soft pretzel for dinner is insurmountable. It's a carb bomb, but whatever, it's freaking delicious and a girl's gotta eat.

There's a lull in the action and the sound of upbeat music blasts through the arena. I realize the song is Macklemore's "Can't Hold Us" and I start nodding my head along to the rhythm. Justin looks up at that exact moment and meets my eyes, grinning at me.

I chuckle and shake my head.

What? I mouth to him. It's a great song.

He no longer has a black eye and he looks so damn good on the ice. His discipline over the offseason has paid off tremendously. The dude is in perfect shape. He simply grins at me once more before skating away to rejoin the pack of players.

Play resumes on the ice as Becca slides back into the seat beside me. I accept the warm pretzel and the stack of napkins she hands me. But then Justin takes a shot and scores, and I'm on my feet, cheering loudly. By the time I remember to take a bite of the pretzel in my hand, it's gone cold.

The guys win the game two to one, and after, Becca and I wait for them to shower and change before we all head out to the nearby bar. Their season is off to an amazing start, and even Becca is in a great mood.

"One drink," I hear her saying beside me as I watch for them.

"That's fine with me."

Owen emerges first. His hair is damp from the shower, and he's dressed in a charcoal gray suit with a black shirt beneath. A huge grin is painted across his features and his blue-gray eyes sparkle with happiness.

Justin is right behind him and the second his gaze meets mine, I fill with nerves. Dear God. This hulking six-foot two of a man who's so bulky and muscled is headed straight toward me. He thrusts a hand through his freshly styled hair and I have to force my eyes away. The perfectly tailored suit he's wearing leaves very little to the imagination, as his powerful thighs carry him toward me, my eyes are drawn briefly to the bulge behind his zipper that hints at an exquisite package. I can barely stop my mouth from watering. My gaze wanders up and I note the way his white button down is open at the collar and the way the navy jacket really brings out his eyes. He looks so hot, but humping him in front of my brother is not an option I can entertain.

When they get closer, Owen lifts Becca into his arms, spinning them both around. She giggles and slaps his shoulder. "Put me down, you big idiot."

He smirks. "We're on fire. Did you see that save I had in the third?"

She nods, and pats his head, looking at Owen warmly. "You did good."

My brother chuckles, watching her with a soft expression.

Becca and I have been friends for four years, and she and Owen have grown close during that time too. It's been pretty much inevitable since we all spend so much time together.

"Nice goal," I say to Justin as we stroll side by side toward the back exit of the arena.

"Thank you," he says casually, lips twitching with a smile.

We pass by a group of female fans who are not at all dressed for the chilly temperatures inside the rink, and I grin as they shoot Becca and I dirty looks. Yes, we're the ones leaving with the guys but we're the furthest thing from puck bunnies you could ever get. Neither of us has ever dated a hockey player. And we probably never will. Becca, because she works here and doesn't want to complicate her work and personal life, and me because of my brother's role on the team.

Once at the bar, we find an empty table and place our order with the server. The guys are always starving after a game and so they order food along with our drinks. Soon Becca and Owen are enthralled in a story about the game, and I listen on while trying not to be distracted by how handsome Justin looks sitting there nursing his beer.

"I'm happy you broke up with Andy," Owen says out of the blue.

"Thanks?" I say. I don't bother pointing out that Andy was the one who broke up with me.

"Yeah, I just think you should stay single. You're young." Owen takes another sip of his beer.

"I could not agree more." Becca nods. Her aversion to relationships is well-known.

Justin stays quiet, and I'm not sure what to think.

"I'm not looking for anything serious, but I wouldn't mind a fling," I say, looking directly at Justin. He doesn't react in any way, and a weird tingling in my stomach makes me feel a little uneasy.

Soon their food is delivered, and they dig in with gusto and I'm thankful the conversation of my love life is forgotten because fries. At least my brother doesn't put up a fight when Becca and I raid his plate for fries.

As promised, Becca and I stay for exactly one drink, which is fine with Owen, because he says he's tired anyways. Justin's hot gaze tracks my every movement, and when I try to pay my tab, he shakes his head.

"Let me." His voice is deep and firm and I find him difficult to say no to, so I nod weakly.

"Thank you." I rise to my feet and shoulder the strap of my purse. Owen helps Becca out of her chair and into her jacket.

Justin remains where he is. "I think I'm going to stick around for a bit."

Owen shoots him a curious glare. "You sure?"

Justin nods. "Yeah. I'm not tired yet."

I assume Owen thinks this is guy code for he's going to stay here and try to score. I pray like hell it's actually him throwing Owen off his trail in case he comes to my place later. But honestly, I'm not exactly sure what to think since we haven't had a moment of privacy all night. I take one last lingering look at Justin and then follow my brother and Becca to the exit.

Outside in the cool night air, Becca and I decide to share a ride home while Owen waves goodnight and gets into his own car.

"What was that about?" Becca asks as soon as we're alone inside the car, her tone practically a hiss.

"I'm not sure," I admit. My phone chirps from inside my purse and I immediately pull it out.

It's a text from Justin.

You want some company tonight?

I swallow, my mouth suddenly dry and flash the screen toward Becca so she can read the text message.

She grins. "What are you going to say?"

"I don't know." I consider his question. "I need to write something flirty."

She nods as my fingers get busy typing.

> That depends.

> On?

> If you're going to stick around tonight or rush out on me in the middle of the action?

> The action? Is that what the kids are calling it these days?

I chuckle at his response as Becca grabs the phone from my hand.

"Let me see," she whines. "I need to live vicariously through you. It's been ages since I've even flirted with a member of the opposite sex. At this point, I wouldn't even remember how."

I don't deny her, letting her take my phone, and soon she's giggling.

"Oh you guys are cute together."

"We're not together," I snap. "We're fuck buddies, Becca. I need to keep that straight."

The driver clears his throat and I can feel my cheeks turning pink.

Whatever.

Come over, I write next.

He sends back: See you in ten.

• • •

I have just enough time to straighten my apartment and brush my teeth when there's a buzz from the intercom system.

He's here.

Butterflies fill my stomach as I head toward the door to let him in.

Recalling the way he set the mood for us last time in his bedroom with the low lighting and the music, I feel a little self-conscious. My apartment isn't romantic or even all that nice, especially not compared to the luxury penthouse he and my brother own.

But once I open the front door, none of that matters. I'm not sure how it's possible, but he looks even better than before. His entire frame fills my doorway, and his features have transformed—his jaw set and chiseled and his eyes are dark with predatory desire.

"Hey," he says softly, looking directly at me. "Can I come in?"

My neck feels warm, like I'm already danger-ously close to blushing, and I step aside, nodding. "Of course."

Justin wanders into my living room and I'm reminded of the last time he was here. We ate ta-cos and then had one of the most monumental con-versations of our entire friendship. Trailing behind him I stuff my hands in my pockets, unsure what else to do with myself.

"Do you … want something to drink? We could watch TV," I offer, voice a little higher than I in-tended.

He turns to face me, his gaze warmly tracking over me. "Come here."

I take three steps and then his strong arms draw me in close to his chest. His masculine scent washes over me as his mouth lowers to mine. His kiss is so soft at first, exploratory and sweet. But then I lift up onto my toes and bring my hands around to the back of his neck, threading them into his hair, and then Justin's lifting me in his arms like I weigh nothing at all.

"I've been waiting a week for that kiss." His voice is husky and I smile, bringing my lips to his again. We kiss again, my lips parting to accept his tongue. I suck it into my mouth and he makes a low noise in his throat.

"Do you want to watch TV?" he asks, a little breathless.

I wrap my legs around his hips and I can feel that he's already hard.

This is moving so much faster than I imagined and I have exactly zero issues with that.

"No," I murmur. "I'm good." In fact, I'm completely fine with the direction this night is heading.

His mouth moves to my neck, which he treats to warm, slow kisses and I practically melt into his arms. It feels so nice.

"Where's your bedroom?" he asks, voice tight.

"Down the hall." I squirm, lifting my chin to give him even better access to my neck.

With purposeful strides, Justin carries me down the short hallway to my room, his lips still at my throat. My heartbeat ratchets up to eight thousand beats per minute.

He lowers me down to the edge of the bed, and suddenly I'm eye level with his groin. I can see the material of his dress pants straining with his excitement.

He looks down at me in amusement. "See something you want?"

I look up and nod at him. "Very much."

Palming him through his pants, I watch for his reaction. His eyes are dark and stormy and filled with want. But he doesn't react, just lets me touch him lightly, squeezing the firm ridge.

When I begin to unbutton his pants, his hands on my wrists stop me. "If you think I'm going to let you do that before I touch you, you're insane."

He releases my wrists, and then draws my shirt off over my head. And then his talented fingers are reaching back and unclasping my bra. It slides down my arms and he drops it beside the bed, his gaze leaving mine to track hotly down my body.

He groans. "You're perfect."

He helps me to my feet, and standing in this position, our height difference is so exaggerated, the top of my head barely clears his chin.

After removing his jacket, his hands span over my ribs and then slide up to cup my breasts. They're small, but perky and he makes a pleased sound as he caresses me.

His mouth latches onto mine, and we kiss deeply for several long moments as he caresses my breasts, lighting pinching my nipples. I feel his touch as though it's between my legs instead of on my breasts, and I give a soft moan.

His lips move to my throat while his hands move down to unbutton my pants. He shoves them down over my hips and then works one hand inside my panties, rubbing me with soft touches that are teasing and gentle and make me hungry for more.

"Mmm … Justin," I moan as my pulse thrums in my veins.

His mouth leaves my neck and he straightens, watching me as he slowly sinks one thick finger inside me. "That feel good?" His voice is so deep and husky. My nipples pebble at the sound of it.

I bite my lower lip, nodding. Clutching his firm biceps while his fingers continue to do magical things to my body, I let out a soft whimper.

"I need a taste," he whispers, pressing one more brief kiss to my damp lips before dropping to his knees on the floor in front of me.

With a hungry look in his eyes, he brings his mouth to my core and treats me to a slow wet lap of his tongue that makes my knees tremble. My thighs part automatically, but I touch his shoulder in protest.

"You don't have to do that…" I groan. "Last time…"

"Last time I enjoyed myself immensely. And I thought you did too," he murmurs, his teeth lightly grazing the soft flesh of my inner thigh.

Oh God. I shudder, remembering what those teeth can do.

"Yes, but I mean you were left …" I wiggle my eyebrows and make a point of looking down at his crotch.

He shakes his head, frowning. "Last time I

abandoned you alone at my apartment while I snuck your brother out like a coward."

Now I'm just confused. I thought that was the right thing to do. At the time, I was nothing but appreciative of his quick thinking. "What else would you have done?"

He shrugs. "I don't know. Man up. Talk to him." His hands skim my hips, and he pulls me down onto the bed so I'm sitting and we're closer to eye-level.

"And say what?" I stare at him, confused. "That we messed up and drunkenly slept together months ago and it almost ruined everything, but now we've decided to just give in to our lust and have a re-do."

He rubs one hand along the back of his neck. "Yeah, it does sound kind of fucking insane when you word it like that."

I chuckle, dryly. "There's no other way to word it. We're friends. With a couple of extra fringe benefits. He does not need to know about this, Justin. He can't."

He's quiet for a moment, and then he nods. "I know. You're right."

Hands sliding along my waist, he reaches one

breast and touches my nipple, lightly pinching it. And the mood I just ruined? Comes roaring back to life.

Justin grabs my thighs and pulls me close. I fall back onto my elbows as he resumes his task from before—teasing me with light licks and kisses against my core.

His hands hold me in place—with my thighs spread for him—and he doesn't stop until I'm panting in pleasure and moving beneath him, rocking my hips into his mouth shamelessly.

"Oh God," I groan, the sound long and throaty.

He looks up at me, mouth still working and smirks. "You keep calling me that and I'm going to develop a complex."

Pushing one hand into his hair, I thrust my hips up, rubbing myself all over his lips and tongue. I'm so close. Right there. And he's fucking teasing me. But then he lightly bites my clit as his finger slides home and I go off like a bottle rocket on the Fourth of July.

Waves of intense pleasure pulse over me, one after the other while Justin watches me from beneath those dark lashes, his finger moving slowly and surely as if to draw out my pleasure. This man knows exactly how to use the gifts God blessed him with.

Finally, the waves subside and I lay back against the bed, body loose and languid. Rising from his spot on the floor, he leans over me, stripping his shirt off so we're bare chest to bare chest. It feels divine.

"You are so sexy when you come." He kisses me deeply while I cling to him, bringing my arms around the tense muscles of his back. "And I was totally kidding before. You can call me God anytime you want."

He rocks into me, letting me feel how hard he is and my body suddenly gets a lot of new ideas.

I kiss him one last time and then meet his eyes with a determined gaze. "Get naked."

He grins. "Yes ma'am."

CHAPTER SIXTEEN

Perfection

Justin

Obeying Elise's command, I strip out of my pants and boxer briefs in about three seconds flat and join her on her bed. I'm so hard and eager, it's almost embarrassing. I'm visualizing my arsenal of mental images to slow this train down— you know, like your grandma at the beach in a bikini or an old man walking out of the sauna at the gym, butt ass naked—to keep myself in check so I can hold out for longer than a teenage boy losing his virginity.

Thankfully Elise doesn't seem to mind. She chews on her lower lip as her gaze tracks down over my chest and abs to where a certain part of my anatomy is more than a little excited to see her.

"Oh," she says, smiling at me, as she reaches one hand out to lightly touch my cock. Even the slightest touches from her feel incredible.

Rubbing her palm along the length of me, Elise moves to my side where she perches on her knees.

Knowing we have all night to enjoy each other, well let's just say, my body has plenty of ideas on exactly how we can spend our time.

She grabs a pillow and puts it behind me. "Lay down," she orders, voice firm but still soft.

I shoot her a curious look. "I didn't know you were so bossy in bed."

She grins. "There are a lot of things you don't know about me."

That is a very true statement. I didn't know that her tits were so perfect that I'll have a hard time ever topping the image of her naked, or that she trembles so hard after she comes that I have to hold her to my chest until her shudders fade.

But, entertained by her, I lay back against the pillow she was thoughtful enough to provide and wait for what happens next.

I cock one eyebrow as I watch her palm me, sizing me up. But she's in no rush, exploring my body with light touches. "What's your plan?" My voice is so husky, but shit, I'm trying to hold it all together. Grandma in a thong ... fuck, that's just wrong. And when she gazes with desire down at my cock again, I know I've lost the battle anyway.

Elise lifts one shoulder, considering my question. "I think I'll start with oral, and then move on to ..."

I place my hand on her upper arm, stroking her silky skin. "You don't have to do that."

She pouts. *She actually fucking pouts.* And my cock grows even harder.

"I mean, I would love for you to, but ..."

She rises her eyebrows, waiting for me to continue.

Oh fuck, she's actually going to make me say it, isn't she?

I clear my throat. "Uh, just. Given my size, that can be difficult."

Unless she's some type of deepthroating expert that I was unaware of.

And honestly? This isn't usually a problem. Most girls aren't interested in blowing me. Once they see my size, and realize it's not going to be easy to get their mouth around me, they just want a ride. Which is always fine with me. More than fine. But Elise's determined expression is fucking adorable. And making me impossibly harder. She tucks her hair efficiently behind her ears and sizes me up, weighing my straining cock in her palms.

I want to laugh and ejaculate at the same time. It's a sensation I've never experienced before. Who knew sex could be so fun, so hot and amusing all at the same time? I'm having a damn good night and we've hardly just begun.

"Just use your hand," I say, fingers skimming over her breasts.

"I want to taste you," she says, a little more shyly this time.

Damn, I love how determined she is. I know I'm not going to deny her.

I stroke one hand through her hair, unable to stop touching her. "I want you to. So badly," I croak out.

"Good. Then we're on the exact same page."

Using both hands, she slowly strokes up my length and lowers her mouth down to my tip at the same time.

So far so good. She's kissing and licking the head and *damn*. It's an explosion of sensations all at once.

She traces her lips down the side, tasting and nibbling as she moves up and down.

I watch her work me over, learning her limits, learning the things that make me groan. It's a wonderful treat to have her hot mouth all over me, and I lay back, one hand buried in her hair, as I turn myself over to the pleasure.

Then she takes me deeper, quickening her pace and my balls start to ache.

Oh sweet fuck. That feels so good.

I can't stop touching her—running my hand along her shoulder, lightly gripping the back of her neck, arranging her hair so it's not in her way—and Elise, *God*, Elise works me to the brink faster than I could have imagined.

"Oh, baby. *Shit*." I let out a sigh of approval.

I'm in heaven. I know I should stop her, I want to be inside her when I come, but it's too good, and it's been so long, and I'm right at the edge, a groan rumbling deep in my chest.

"Fuck, fuck, *fuck. Elise.*"

I cannot come in her mouth. I have enough guilt about this entire thing. I can't let myself do that on top of everything else. It feels like a sin I am not quite ready to commit.

I pull her mouth away just in time, and using both hands, she strokes me firmly as I come all over us both.

"Damn, girl," I groan, somehow out of breath though I've done nothing but lay here. I pull her down for a kiss.

Elise giggles at my praise, kissing me back—on my lips, jaw, my chin. And then she paints one delicate finger through the sticky mess, a smile on her lips.

"Sorry about that." I look down at the mess on my stomach.

"Are you kidding? I loved doing that for you." And her sincerity is genuine—it's written all over her face.

My heart squeezes in my chest. I kiss her once more and then I do the post-sex walk into her bathroom that's normally so awkward, but it somehow feels different with her. It feels natural, and somehow just, real.

After I wipe up and wash my hands, I re-join her on the bed. She's pulled back the sheets and is lounging comfortably against the pillows. And best of all, she's still naked.

"You look perfect like that. Don't move." I take a moment to admire her before I slip in beside her.

She puts one hand on my cheek and turns my face toward hers.

"That was amazing," she murmurs.

Part of me wants to make some cocky re-mark—*you ain't seen nothing yet, baby*—but the other part of me is speechless, because she's right. That was—different. Amazing in its own way. I think because it was *us*. And that scares me more than anything. So I don't say anything at all.

Instead, I turn her chin toward mine and kiss her softly. "Give me fifteen minutes and I'll be ready again."

Elise bites her lip, looking uncertain, but then she straddles me, her warm, wet pussy rubbing over the length of my semi-erect dick, and brushes the tops of her breasts against my chest.

My body reacts to hers immediately. *Holy hell.*

"Actually, scratch that. I won't need that long."

Elise chuckles while I reach over the side of the bed, hunting for my pants until I locate the condoms I brought.

I rip one off the string of linked packets and tear open the package. I only brought two with me so I wouldn't be tempted to push her for more and make her sore. I move back to our previous positions, so we're laying side by side, facing each other. It's extremely intimate and a little unnerving. I might have had sex countless times with many women, but there's no denying, this is somehow different.

Her wide, blue-gray eyes are locked onto mine as I roll the condom down my shaft, wincing a little at the tight fit. I fucking hate condoms, but what are you going to do?

She's beautiful. And so tempting. But she's also so pure, and inexperienced. I know I need to take my time and make this good for her. The last thing I want to do is hurt her. I take a deep breath, and force myself to slow down.

Normally, sex for me is a quick and meaningless affair. A primal release. Something that offers little in the way of emotional satisfaction. But with

Elise? Everything I've ever known flies out the window.

I meet her eyes, and touch her cheek with my fingertips, checking to be sure she's okay. "Hey," I murmur.

She swallows, visibly. "Hey." Her voice is a little breathless, and I get the sense she's nervous.

"Are you alright?"

She nods. "I'm alright. I guess I'm just a little anxious about this hurting."

It's then that I realize she may not have had sex with anyone else since we were together. It's an idea I never entertained before. It's been months. Even though I hated the idea of it, I had resigned myself to the fact she was most-likely sleeping with that guy she started seeing.

And even though I want to punch myself for this question, it falls from my lips before I can help it.

"Am I the only man you've been with?"

She chews on her lower lip, stalling. "Umm?"

"Elise."

"Yes."

Fuck. That secret knowledge does something to me.

"Is…is that okay?" she breathes.

Oh my fuck. I can't with this girl. Knowing I'm the only man who's been inside her? Knowing it's only my cock that has stretched her? Knowing she's going to be so tight I can hardly breathe? Um, yeah. It's more than *okay*. It's fucking amazing.

Instead, I find myself softening.

"I just don't want to hurt you," I hear myself say. And it's the complete truth.

She swallows. "You won't. I want you. So bad." She lifts one leg, and places her thigh over the top of mine.

I move closer, and grip myself with one hand, rubbing the head of my cock along her tight seam until Elise is moaning and trembling.

I hate myself for it, because I'm sure it's going to be uncomfortable for her at the very least, but I can't fucking wait to get inside her.

"Tell me if I do something you don't like, or you need a break, or if you want to stop…"

My voice is cut off by her low moan, and she

reaches down, taking me in her hand to guide me to her opening herself. "I want you, Justin…now," she repeats.

Holding her top thigh with one hand, keeping her open for me, my other hand touches her breast, my thumb skimming lightly over her nipple.

Pushing my hips forward, I sink inside so slowly and we release a simultaneous groan. I try like hell to not blow my load at how she fits me like a fucking glove.

"Can you handle a little more?" I ask.

Her eyes sink closed, and she arches, pushing her pelvis closer. "Yes. More."

She feels so warm and so wet and so perfect, I can't hold myself back any longer.

I sink deeper until I'm fully buried within her tight heat and then I still, watching her reaction. Elise's lips part, and her eyes fall closed. She makes a little shuddering sigh sound.

I'd forgotten how amazing it feels to be inside her. I'd forgotten how desperate and alive she makes me feel, how every tight squeeze of her sends a jolt of pleasure rushing through me.

Careful not to hurt her or rush through this, I set

an easy pace, moving in slow, even strokes. I can't stop touching her—running my fingers through her silky hair, caressing her soft skin.

"Does it feel okay to you?" she asks, eyes half-lidded as she watches me move in long, lazy strokes.

I touch her cheek, bringing her lips to mine. "Nothing has ever felt this good."

It's the complete truth.

She reaches between us to touch herself, her fingers brushing where we're joined.

"Oh fuck yes," I groan. "That's it." I love watching her take what she needs. I love how un-inhibited she is.

I need to make this a lot better than her first time, and so far I think we're on our way.

Increasing our tempo, I drive into her faster, and Elise starts to moan.

"Oh God. Justin…."

Her body tightens around my shaft, and I can feel her trembling. She's so close.

I groan at how good she feels squeezing the shit out of me. My eyes are glued to her, I love watching her. I wish we could do this all night, but I know it's going to be over way too fast. My groin is already throbbing with the need to empty myself inside of her.

With a low moan, Elise lets go, her body rhythmically milking mine as waves of pleasure crash through her. I gather her into my arms, my face in her neck as I continue pumping into her. Her whole body is shaking as I pull her up on top of me. She straddles my hips, and she's draped across my chest. I lift her hips up and down over me, moving faster, chasing my own release now.

I worry for a second that I'm being too rough, but Elise's whimpers and throaty moans tell me she's enjoying this as much as I am.

Each time I thrust up, I praise her. "You're so tight. So perfect. You feel so good."

And then I'm coming again—erupting into the condom in hot spurts—and holding her close as little tremors and aftershocks wreck her body.

Perfection.

That was perfection.

CHAPTER SEVENTEEN

French Toast and French Kisses

Elise

Waking up next to Justin feels a little surreal. I can still remember him with bright red cheeks and hockey skates in his hands. I remember a million shared laughs and mugs of hot cocoa. But I have exactly zero memories of him like *this*. With messy, sex-styled hair and his chiseled features relaxed in sleep.

I've never done the whole one-night stand thing, and honestly I'm not sure of the proper protocol. He's still asleep, and not wanting to wake him, I decide to slip out of bed. In the bathroom, I brush my teeth and brush the tangles from my hair.

Last night after we'd had sex, we'd lounged in bed together for a while until his stomach growled. Then he hunted through my kitchen for something to eat. We'd brought our snacks to the living room and watched TV for a little while. Then he'd borrowed a toothbrush and we'd gone to bed together, me curled up in his strong arms, my head resting against his sculpted chest. I smile at the memory. This is exactly what I'd wanted—to chase away the regret of our first time together, and I think I've succeeded.

After I finish in the bathroom, I tiptoe beside the bed with the plan to go to the kitchen to start a pot of coffee. I'm sure he needs his sleep. He had a game last night and then we played sex Olympics until the early morning hours, so he must be exhausted. But he catches me as I move by the bed, one strong arm snaking out to grab me around the waist and haul me back to bed. I land with a soft grunt right on top of him.

He's smiling. "Hey."

I grin. "Hi."

He's wearing boxer briefs and I can feel that he's hard when he rolls me onto my back, supporting his weight over me on his forearms.

He kisses my lips and then pulls back with an amused expression. "You brushed your teeth?"

I nod. "I was planning to let you sleep."

He looks so relaxed and happy, and not at all self-conscious about what we did last night. He's probably much more well-versed in the art of the one-night stand than I am. It's a thought that stings a little.

"I'm up," he says, eyes crinkling in the corners as he watches me.

"I can tell," I say, smirking at him. I'm referring to the hard ridge pressed right up against my stomach.

Justin chuckles, and gives his hips a slow roll. "You want to fuck again?"

"Oh my God," I laugh, shaking my head. "*That's* how you ask me?"

With an amused expression, he rocks his hips into me again. "I want you." His voice is warm, and husky, and believe me, I'm tempted, even if a romantic he is *not*.

"I'm a little sore," I admit. A look of concern flashes across his features. "But it's the good kind of sore. And I have brunch plans with the girls."

"Oh. Okay." He blinks at me, and then rolls to his side, freeing me a second later.

"I'm going to go make us some coffee," I announce, rising from the bed.

I pretend not to notice his confused expression as I shuffle from the room. Of course I wish I could just jump back into bed and have sex with him again, but I also know that I have to protect myself from developing any expectations. After all this is just casual sex. And I have to put a little distance between us right now to stop myself from feeling anything.

I have the coffee started and two mugs set out on the counter when he emerges from my bedroom, now fully dressed in his dress pants and button-down shirt from last night. His feet are bare, and I have no idea why I find that so hot, but I do.

I pour him a mug of coffee, and hand it to him. I guess this is one perk of our long-standing friendship, I know exactly how he takes his coffee.

"Thanks." His deep voice rumbles low, and I smile, amused.

Not for the first time, I think about how glad I am that we're doing this, that we've patched up our friendship, and now there are orgasms involved.

"So, what's on your agenda this week?" I ask, sipping my coffee.

He rubs one hand through his hair. "The usual. Practice. A team meeting on Wednesday. A game this weekend. You?"

I shrug. "Just work and plans with Becca later this week."

"Can I see you again?"

Smiling behind my coffee mug, I nod.

He steps closer, closing me in against the kitchen counter. "Is that a yes?"

"Yes," I murmur as he takes the mug from my hands and sets it on the counter behind me.

Then he places my hands on his chest, and puts his hands on my jaw, and then we're kissing again. I taste a hint of coffee as his tongue strokes mine. After a moment, he pulls back, touching his thumb to my lower lip. "I better go. Have fun with the girls."

"I will."

He shoves his feet into his shoes, and gives me one last quick kiss goodbye at the door.

"I'll text you later," he says as he heads out and I nod.

It's pouring rain outside and he's got no raincoat, so he makes a dash for his car, waving at me as he climbs inside.

• • •

A big plate of French toast appears in front of me and I inhale the smell of sweet batter and powdered sugar.

"Okay, now I'm officially jealous," Bailey groans, looking at my plate in envy.

I nod to the egg whites and wheat toast the waitress has placed in front of her. "Yes, but that's so much healthier. I'm sure I'll regret this in about an hour." Even as I say the words, I know it's not true. Nothing can mess with my mood today.

Sara and Becca both ordered the avocado toast, which is what I usually get too at our favorite breakfast spot. But after all the calories I burned last night, I wanted to splurge—or celebrate, maybe a little of both.

It was an amazing night, and I'm still on a post-orgasmic high. I cut one triangle of French toast in half and slide it onto Bailey's plate. "Here. Please don't let me eat all this myself."

She flashes me a grin. "Done."

"You guys missed a good game last night," Becca says to Bailey and Sara, but her gaze cuts over to me and she winks.

I know she's dying to know what happened between Justin and I last night.

"They won, right?" Bailey asks. Being good friends with the team means we have the best seats, and we usually all attend together, but last night it was just Becca and I.

Sara nods. "Yeah. Teddy was texting me, telling me to come out and meet them at the bar, but I wasn't in the mood to deal with the puck bunnies drooling all over them. It gets so old, you know?"

"So old," Becca confirms. "But last night Owen and Justin were actually behaving themselves. We grabbed one beer after the game, and then Owen went home alone. I'm not sure about Justin though." She looks at me again, clearly baiting me.

I stuff another bite of French toast into my mouth and focus on chewing, and not making eye contact because Becca can read me like a damn book.

"That sounds like a first for Owen then. And I can guarantee you Justin wasn't lonely last night. They're both manwhores," Bailey says.

I swallow my food and take a sip of mimosa. "They're not that bad."

Sara laughs, pointing her fork at me. "You're just in denial because Owen is your brother and you love him, but *girl*." She shakes her head. "They are worse than *that bad*. Teddy is, well, Teddy, and he went all TMI on me last time we went out. About how they're all on Tinder before the plane even touches down during away games. How they have strategies to sneak girls into the hotel, even if it's past curfew. Trust me. They sleep around with as much enthusiasm as they play hockey."

Bailey launches into a story about Justin getting head from one girl while he made out with another at a club last year, and I suddenly feel sick.

I drain the last of my mimosa and set the empty glass down a little harder than I intended to.

Becca gazes at me with a look of sympathy.

"Alright guys, that's enough," Becca warns. "I'm sure Elise doesn't want to hear these kinds of stories about her brother."

Sara takes another bite, shaking her head. "We weren't talking about Owen. We were talking about Justin."

Bailey makes a noise of disagreement. "Yes but Justin's practically like a brother to Elise too."

Um, no.

Not even close.

No longer hungry, I push my plate away, and when the waitress approaches, I order a second mimosa. I'm not sure why I'm so upset. None of what they've said is new information to me. I guess it's just that I have no idea if we're exclusive and if we're not, I don't want to do this if we're not. I don't want feelings involved but I also don't want to sleep with him if he's still sleeping around when he's on the road. I've been hurt by him before and it would crush me to know that I'm nothing but a number to him, someone to warm his bed on the off-nights that he's not taking a puck bunny home.

Obviously the champagne has gone to my head, because I fish my phone out of my purse, and compose a text to him under the table.

> You know what, I changed my mind about this week.

> I don't want to do this anymore.

His reply comes in a few seconds later.

Why? Did I do something wrong?

I scoff, and set my cell in my lap. I don't want to start a fight with him right now. I don't want to talk about any of this. The truth is, my girlfriends are right. He gets so much regular sex, my absence in his bed won't matter. He'll hardly even notice it. The anger simmering under the surface rises to a low boil. I can't believe I thought this idiotic plan would ever work. I close my eyes and draw a deep breath, deciding on a simple, straight-forward reply.

I can't talk right now.

Bailey and Becca are talking about seeing the new rom com that's releasing in theaters this week, and I mumble something about joining them. But I'm so distracted. And now pissed off. I feel my phone vibrate and I look down to see another text from him.

If this is what you want, I'll respect your decision. But we're going to talk about this.

I roll my eyes, my fingers flying over the keys

as I reply.

> I'd rather not be exposed to
> whatever you pick up from all
> the women in your bed.

After several seconds of silence, I assume he's not going to text me back, mostly likely because he's got no come-back for that. Which only makes me feel worse, because it means I'm right. I didn't want to be right. But at least I found this out now before I got in too deep.

But then my phone is ringing. I look down. He's calling me. Why the hell is he calling me right now?

I hit ignore and send the call to voicemail. Becca is watching me, obviously wondering what the hell is going on. My phone starts vibrating again, and I slide from the booth, with the excuse of needing to go to the bathroom.

In the back hallway near the restrooms, I answer my phone.

"Yes?" I say, tone clipped.

I hear a door closing, and I picture him going into his bedroom to get privacy away from Owen.

"Elise? What the hell is going on?" he says, tone filled with confusion.

"You tell me." I place one hand on my hip, waiting for his reply. It feels like so long ago that we were in my kitchen, kissing and drinking coffee and making plans.

"I don't know what you think this is between us," he says. "But while we're doing this, I have no plans to be with anyone else. And I get tested regularly. The whole team does."

And now I feel bad because I never meant to imply that he had a sexually transmitted disease, I was just frustrated over the thought of being one of many. Even if we are just messing around, it's still a big deal to me.

I lick my lips and take a deep breath. "What are you saying? Are we exclusive? We're just messing around right? It wouldn't be fair to expect that of you."

He lets out a tense breath. "Let me help you understand this. First, hell yes we're exclusive. For whatever this is and however long it lasts, I'm not fucking anyone but you. And you're sure as hell not fucking anyone else either."

The knot in my stomach suddenly eases. "Oh,

okay."

"Okay? We're good then?" he says.

"Yeah."

Justin chuckles, the sound warm and soft and all the tension melts away. "Are you still at brunch?"

"Yes. And I better, um, go."

He makes a sound of disagreement. "We're going to talk more about this."

"Justin…" I plead, gazing back at our table.

"I'm serious, Elise. The next time I see you I want to know who or what got into your head and made you think you were just a casual fuck buddy to me. I've known you for damn near my entire life. Don't you think that means something?"

My stomach swarms with butterflies and I nod, before realizing I've gone entirely mute. "I ---"

"You're going to tell me, and if you don't, I have ways of getting the information out of you, you know."

"Okay, we can talk later, but I really do have to go." Before I do or say anything else to embarrass myself. And with that, I hang up and stuff my phone in my back pocket to re-join my girlfriends at the table.

CHAPTER EIGHTEEN

The Chase

Justin

"**S**he's worried she's going to turn into a crazy old cat lady," Owen says, frowning.

I pause, weighing his words as my brain scrambles to catch up. "Who are we talking about again?" To say I'm a little distracted would be a massive understatement.

"Becca," he says with a tone that asks if I've been following his story at all.

Shit. After finishing my last rep, I set the weights that I've been lifting down and heave out an exhale. "Does she even own a cat?"

"Nope," Owen confirms, grabbing two forty-pound dumbbells and taking a seat on the bench beside mine. "I told her that it's fucking ridiculous."

I knew only a little bit of Becca's history. It wasn't something she liked to broadcast to our friend group, but I knew she was a sexual assault survivor. The keyword there was *survivor*. Owen once said the word *victim* in Elise's presence, and she almost castrated him.

Becca seemed normal enough. She wasn't timid around men, at least not within our group of friends, but apparently she hadn't been out on a date in two years and Owen had called her on it. Which led to them having a whole discussion, which leads to this moment where Owen is replaying the entire thing to me while we work out.

I grab my towel from the bench and wipe the sweat from the back of my neck.

His story is a welcome distraction, because I've spent the last several days replaying my time with Elise like a song on repeat.

I may be at the gym inside our training facility, but my mind? It's still firmly on last Saturday night, the night I spent in Elise's bed. I can't stop thinking about her soft skin, or the way she felt in my arms, or the things she can do with her mouth... I've thought about that a lot too, specifically in the frequent showers I've been taking since last Saturday.

I've also been replaying that weird conversation we had, and the fact that she compared herself to a random hookup.

I haven't had the chance to see her since then. She's been busy with work and other personal commitments. Part of me is a little thrown off by this. To be honest I'm not used to women being too busy to see me, or turning me down for sex—which she did the morning we woke up together. Granted maybe she really was too sore, but somehow I don't think that's the whole story.

Elise isn't some fan-girl who drools all over me, or idolizes the ground I walk on. In a way, it's been refreshing to be told no. She doesn't care who I am, or what I can do with a stick and a six-ounce disk of hard rubber. I'm just Justin to her. She's doing this on her terms, and it only makes me want to chase her more.

Owen is still talking, and I'm trying like hell to listen, but the memory of my conversation with Elise about exclusivity pops into my head and I have to hold in a chuckle. I still haven't gotten the story of exactly why that topic came up, but I have a feeling there was something said during brunch with her girlfriends that made her go all posses-sive-territorial over my cock. And fuck if I don't like that. It's all hers, she can have it for as long as she wants it. There is no one else I want more than Elise, which made it very easy to agree to her terms. Plus, the thought of her with another man? Fuck that. I want to be the one to please her, and spend time with her, and provide all the orgasms she can handle.

"You done?" Owen asks, standing over me.

I'm pretty sure I spaced out five minutes ago and have just been laying on the mat rather than stretching. I straighten and sit up. "Yeah, I'm good."

I grab my towel and my water bottle and we make our way to the showers.

After stripping down, we grab a few towels from the stack and each head into a shower stall. Each shower is divided by a half-wall, so the tops and bottoms are open.

Owen tests the water before stepping in, while I crank mine to the hottest it will go and ease myself under the spray.

"I texted Elise and invited her over for dinner tonight. You going to be around?" Owen asks as I rub shampoo into my hair.

I will now. "Yeah. Sure." I silently congratulate myself on my casual tone. Even if I hate the idea of sneaking around Owen to get to Elise, at least for right now, it's a necessity.

On the way home, Owen's driving, so I fire off a quick text to Elise.

```
I hear you're coming for dinner
tonight.
```

It only takes her a few seconds to reply.

```
Owen talked me in to cooking.
       Are you going to be home?
```

I shoot back. `I'll eat anything you spread in front of me. :)`

Back at home, I tidy up my bedroom, even though it's a slim chance in hell Elise will even see it. But still, I have a girl coming over. A girl I like very much. Even if she is Owen's sister, a man can hope.

We'd texted all week trying to make plans to

see each other before I fly out to the Midwest for the next couple of days, but so far, this appears to be our best and maybe only opportunity.

Too bad we have a freaking chaperone tonight.

Owen runs to the grocery store, and I have this secret fantasy that he'll still be gone when Elise arrives, but no such luck. He returns with three bags of groceries which I help him unload on the counters. We usually take turns shopping so everything stays fair. There's ground beef, onion, garlic, dried pasta and all the fixings for salad.

"Italian?" I ask, removing two bottles of red wine from the last bag.

"Yeah. I asked Elise to make our mom's recipe for lasagna. I've been craving it for weeks."

"Cool." I knew Elise could cook. She occasionally gets talked into making something for Owen, but I find myself cataloging this information away as just one more thing I like about her. The thought of her all domestic in the kitchen, feeding me is a happy one. Owen and I spent way too much time eating out, especially while on the road.

Elise arrives a short time later, knocking once and then letting herself inside. "Hey," she says, smiling as she enters. She's dressed in a pair of black leggings and an oversized sweatshirt with the name of the school she teaches at emblazoned across the front. The idea of her wrangling a group of chaotic four-year-olds is one that also makes me smile. She's got the whole nurturing thing down to a science…both with the little kids she works with and within our friend circle.

She removes her rainboots at the door and then heads inside. With only a passing glance at me, she greets Owen, giving him a hug.

"What am I making?" she asks.

He chuckles. "Mom's lasagna."

She grins and rubs her hands together. "Yum. Okay. It'll take a while though. Can you wait?"

Owen nods. "I bought wine. And I can make salad and breadsticks. So yeah, we are good."

Elise nods and then takes one more glance my way, her eyes lingering on mine, longer this time. "Hey, Justin."

"Hello, Elise." Her name comes out deeper than I intended.

Fuck, this feels weird.

I can only hope Owen has no idea how formal

and awkward we sound. I'd give anything to go up to her and kiss her, but instead I take a seat at one of the barstools at the counter.

Owen uncorks a bottle of wine and pours three glasses.

I accept mine and take a sip. "What can I help with?" I ask.

Elise surveys her surroundings, cataloging the items Owen's brought home. Then she grabs a wooden cutting board and places it in front of me. "Can I trust you with a chef's knife?"

I don't cook. And apparently Elise knows this.

"I think so, I mean, I can catch and control a puck with the edge of a wooden stick traveling at a hundred miles an hour, so lay it on me."

She chuckles and then grabs the lettuce and the vegetables for the salad. "Then why don't you get to work on this?"

"I can handle that."

We exchange one more look before Elise gets busy. Owen has retreated to the other side of the kitchen and is placing frozen breadsticks onto a baking sheet, which means I get to watch Elise and hopefully not cut my damn fingers off.

She chops an onion while the beef browns in a skillet on the gas range. The oven is preheating and a mixture of tomatoes and garlic simmers over another burner.

She's certainly comfortable in the kitchen, and I like watching her work much more than I thought I would. I was half-worried that tonight would be torture—an exercise in look but don't touch—a concept I'm not very good at. But I'm having more fun than I expected.

"What else can I do?" Owen asks, taking a sip of his wine as he surveys our progress.

Elise glances around the kitchen. "I'm done with that sauté pan if you want to wash it. Otherwise, I think we're good."

Following her orders, Owen grabs the pan and takes it to the sink where he begins scrubbing it with hot, soapy water.

Elise and I are quiet, and I sense she wishes it was just the two of us almost as badly as I do. Once the sauté pan has been washed and dried, Owen retreats to the couch with his glass of wine and the sports highlights to keep him company.

I finish the salad prep with no bloodshed, but since I'm not ready to leave the kitchen, I grab my phone and pretend to be scrolling through social media while I'm watching Elise's ass as she moves around the kitchen. There's something about her dressed in leggings that my cock likes way too much. The stretchy black material leaves very little to the imagination. When she reaches up to grab a dish on the top shelf, my gaze tracks down over the curve of her soft hips.

I know I'm torturing myself, but damn, I love her body.

Once Elise has everything under control, she picks up her wineglass and takes a long drink. I get the sense that she's purposefully avoiding looking my direction. She grabs three plates from the cabinet and the silverware from a drawer. Once everything is on the table and the timer is set, Elise heads into the living room.

I follow her, taking a seat on the couch beside Owen, and directly across from her.

Owen and Elise are discussing Becca in low tones while I pretend to dick around on my phone some more. Who knew it would be this difficult pretending?

I'm struck by a sudden realization. I don't just like all the physical stuff with her, I like just hanging out with her too. I guess it's not all that strange, I've been friends with her for so long. But I guess it's the first time I can picture myself being in a real relationship, picture myself having a girlfriend. Picture myself wanting more. And for once, the thought of being tied down doesn't give me hives. I can imagine us cooking together, cuddling on the couch while dinner simmers in the kitchen.

"Are you seeing anyone new?" Owen asks her, drawing me from my private thoughts.

Elise shakes her head. "No. I just want to keep things casual for a while. I'm young, you know? I don't want to tie myself down to one man."

Owen nods. "Smart." His eyes leave the TV and meet hers. "You are young. I wouldn't want to see you get all serious with the first real relationship you have."

Elise is staring straight ahead at the TV, and I'd give anything to know what she's thinking. "I totally agree. I'm all about casual these days."

Her remarks have left me feeling slightly unsettled, but I can't put my finger on why.

Finally, it's time to eat, and we help ourselves to generous portions of the meal. It looks and smells amazing.

Elise compliments me on the salad while both Owen and I praise her on the lasagna. We polish off one bottle of wine, but no one's in the mood to open the second.

"A night in to eat, relax," Owens says, standing up from the table and wrapping one hefty arm over Elise's slim shoulders. "You're freaking awesome, sis."

Her eyes dart to mine, and then stray over to this. "I am pretty amazing."

I laugh at this and they both look at me. "I'll, um, start the dishes."

Heading toward the kitchen, I grab our empty plates on the way. Elise follows her brother into the living room. She somehow managed to clean up as she cooked so there's not much to do besides put our dishes into the dishwasher, which only takes me a couple of minutes.

When I'm finished, I hear Elise telling Owen that she needs to go to the restroom before heading out.

It's been maddening to be this close to her, yet still be so far away. Taking a chance, I follow her, opening the bathroom door and slipping in behind her.

Her eyes go wide and her cheeks flush pink. "What are you doing in here?" she whispers.

I don't answer. Instead I take two steps, closing the distance between us, and pull her into my arms at the same time my mouth finds hers. Her lips part and a squeak of surprise rises in her throat. Her eager tongue strokes mine and I have to brace one hand against the bathroom sink to keep my knees from trembling. She tastes like wine and her fingers dig into my biceps as I push my hips up against hers.

Almost as fast as I dared come in here and kiss her, I leave, my heart beating fast and my cock swelling against my thigh.

Later when it's time for Elise to go, it's physically painful to pretend I'm so unaffected. But I have to. From my spot on the couch, I give a half-wave. "Dinner was fun. See ya."

Elise smiles once and then follows Owen to the door where she puts on her boots one at a time, chuckling at something he's said.

I want to hug her, and kiss her goodnight, or you know, drag her to my bedroom like a cave-man and make love to her all night. But instead, I do what's expected of me and ignore them as they part ways.

I have no idea what it is about this woman that gets me so worked up, but I intend to find out.

CHAPTER NINETEEN

Playtime

Elise

*W*here is he?

I glance at the clock again and silently curse Owen. Cursing *silently* is a necessity right now since I'm standing in the middle of my pre-school classroom. Owen was supposed to be here fifteen minutes ago for Career Day, but so far, he's a no-show.

"Miss Parrish?" a little voice asks. It comes out sounding more like *Paris*, but hey when you're four years old, it's the best you can do.

"Yes, Britton?" I ask, looking down to ruffle the adorable little guy's hair.

"Fireman?" he asks with hope-filled blue eyes gazing up at mine.

I shake my head. "We already had the fireman come this morning, and then the police officer, and then the dentist, remember?"

He waves his new red toothbrush at me. "I remember."

"Good. Now please go sit back down for circle time. We have one more guest coming to talk about his job."

I can only stall a classroom of antsy toddlers for so long, and we passed that threshold about twelve minutes ago. If Owen doesn't show in the next few seconds, I guess we'll have to cut Career Day short and move onto something easy, yet stimulating. I'm thinking my extra special gooey dough. Even if I'll probably end up having to wash chunks of it from my hair tonight, the kids love that glittery, messy concoction. It might be my only option since I didn't plan for this scenario.

Crossing the room toward my desk, I grab my phone from inside the top drawer and glance down at a text from Owen that was sent over an hour ago.

Not going to make it. Sorry, sis!

I groan. *Shit. Now what?*

I rarely get the chance to check my phone during the work day so I'm just now seeing his message. I have no idea what happened, but I intend to find out later.

Well onto plan B then I guess. I'm mentally tallying if I have all the ingredients I need to make the homemade play-dough when I realize I'm going to have a bunch of disappointed little kids because they'd been so excited when I told them a player from the Seattle Ice Hawks was going to be here today.

Ugh.

I turn to face my class, and take a deep breath. I'm just about to muster a false cheery tone to tell them Owen's visit has been cancelled when my classroom door opens.

And in walks Justin, dressed in full game-day gear. Minus the skates, of course.

My eyes widen at the sight of him. His hockey bag is slung over one shoulder and he's holding his stick in his left hand. His eyes lock with mine and I'm sure a look of confusion is painted across my features, because what in the heck is he doing here? He gives me a lopsided smile and my insides tighten.

Applause and cheers break out among the kids as he heads straight for the front of the class.

He gives me a wink as he passes by, and then stops directly in front of the circle time rug.

"Hi, guys. I heard you were talking about careers today. Is it okay if I join you?"

Little Elsa raises her hand and Justin nods for her to go ahead.

"What is your job?" she asks, eyes wide as she takes in the sight of him.

He chuckles, the sound immediately releasing the knot of nerves I felt when Owen cancelled. My shoulders drop a few inches and I take a deep breath, hoping Justin has this covered. Just please don't drop any F-bombs, I silently pray.

"I play hockey," Justin says, giving her a wink.

I clear my throat and go to stand next to him. "Class, this is Justin Brady, number thirty-six, and the star forward of the Seattle Ice Hawks. Can everyone say hi?"

"Hiii, Mista Bwady," rings a chorus of little voices.

I look to see Justin's reaction, but he's focused

on me. His head is tilted and he's staring down at me with a look of adoration. "Hi," he says softly.

I blush, heat creeping up my neck and over my cheeks. "Hello," I manage. "Thanks for coming."

He nods once, mouth quirking up in a smirk. I can tell he wants to kiss me. But I hope that he can tell I'll knee him in the nuts if he does that in front of my class.

Justin and I are just standing here staring at each other, obviously flirting and the sound of giggles around us pull me back to reality. Okay then. Right. Career Day. Not the day to hump the sexy-ass hockey player in front of my class.

Recovering, I draw another breath. "Today Justin is going to tell us what it's like to have a job as a hockey player."

I motion for him to go ahead and begin when Elsa raises her hand again.

"Yes, Elsa?"

"Don't you mean Mister Bwady?"

I swallow a lump the size of the state of Washington and nod. "Yes. I'm sorry, Mr. Brady."

Justin smiles again and then drops his hockey

bag to his feet with a loud thump. "Show of hands ... who here has ever watched a hockey game?"

All of the little hands dart up and wave around excitedly.

"That's awesome." Justin nods. Then he holds up his hockey stick. "And who knows what this is?"

"A hockey stick!" Britton calls out.

"That's right. Wow. Very good."

I grin, watching them, so thankful that Justin stepped in and saved the day. And so far, so good.

"And what about this?" Justin toes the huge black bag at his feet. "What do you think this bag contains?"

One of my most quiet and shy little boys, Jacob raises his hand to answer. "Your hockey equipment."

Justin nods. "You're right. Very smart. What a great class. I see Miss Parrish has taught you all well."

Jacob beams under the praise, lowering his head as a big, proud smile overtakes his face. It's adorable. Even if Justin doesn't know it, I think he just made Jacob's entire day. Maybe his whole week.

And I shake my head, smiling at the compliment he paid me. Despite what Justin might think, I don't teach them about hockey. I'm sure they learn it from their parents and TV and well, everywhere considering the Ice Hawks are worshiped like gods in this city.

Justin fills them in on his practice and training schedule, the away games they attend and all the hard work needed to succeed as a hockey player. The kids are mesmerized by him. They hang on his every word, and nod along with his explanations. I never knew he could be so good with kids. Then again, as a pro athlete, I'm sure he's done these kinds of things before. Only I'm guessing they were official visits to children's hospitals and things like that, arranged by the team publicist. Either way, he's doing great.

Then he kneels down to the floor, joining them at their level as he unzips his hockey bag. I expect to see his helmet, hockey pucks, rolls of tape, and his pads. Instead, it's been filled to the brim with promotional items from the team. Hats, buttons, plastic cups, stickers, foam hockey pucks, t-shirts, and Justin tosses item after item to the excited little grabby hands reaching out toward him. Delighted squeals and giggles erupt through my classroom as all the goodies are handed out.

The dentist had brought toothbrushes and floss picks, the fireman had brought stickers and the policeman was cool simply because he had a gun and handcuffs and the kids were wide-eyed amazed. But Justin, handing out dozens of goodies is just too much for them to contain their excitement. Soon, he's being high-fived and tackle-hugged and one thing leads to another, and there are like three kids climbing him like he's the new play structure equipment.

I can't hold in my laughter as Justin rises to his feet with one little boy riding on his shoulders, and two more draped across each of his bulky arms. Elsa wraps herself around one muscular leg and then Jacob does the same with his other leg. How he can even walk with five little bodies attached to him, I have no idea, but he does, slowly lumbering across the room amidst delighted squeals of laughter.

I didn't think anyone would top the fireman's visit, but clearly I thought wrong. Justin is a hit. I can tell I'm going to have a hard time wrangling them and reining in their disappointment when it's time for him to leave. Which will be soon, because I'm sure he's got better things to do today than wrestle a half dozen toddlers, as adorable as it is.

After a few more minutes of play, I decide it's time to break up the fun. "Okay friends, I think it's time for us to say goodbye to Mr. Brady and thank him for coming."

There are a few disappointed groans as the kids release him, and even a couple of tears as I have to physically remove Elsa from his leg. Trust me, girlfriend, I get it. I really do. The guy is dreamy as fuck.

The kids thank Justin for coming, and he thanks them for letting him play, which melts me just a little further.

After he gathers his gear back up, he heads toward the door, lingering there for a moment like he has something he wants to say.

"Class, please line up at the sinks and begin washing your hands for snack. I'll be right back."

As Justin steps into the hall, I linger by the door, watching him.

"What was all this? Did Owen send you?" I ask, sure to keep my voice quiet.

He meets my eyes, and *oh my God*, I can tell again that he wants to kiss me. I cannot let that happen, no matter how tempting an offer that is.

"Owen didn't send me. I heard him on the phone with the team trainer. He was called in for a meeting today and he was complaining about how it conflicted with coming to visit your class. In the end, he figured you would understand, and they didn't seem to be giving him much of a choice."

"So … what? You just had nothing better to do than spend your morning getting climbed like a jungle gym by half a dozen toddlers?" I ask in a challenging tone, raising one eyebrow to watch him.

His eyebrows pull together. "Are you mad I'm here?"

"No." I wave my hands. "Not at all. I'm sorry. I'm grateful you're here. Let me start over. Thank you for coming. Honestly. You saved my … *backside*. I'm just confused, I guess on how this all transpired."

He licks his lips, and places one hand against my shoulder, lightly squeezing. "I wouldn't have come unless I wanted to."

A quick glance inside my classroom shows me

that they're halfway through washing hands and I only have another fifteen seconds at best, even though I could happily spend all day gazing up at his chiseled jaw and gorgeous blue eyes.

"Thank you, Justin. Honestly."

His mouth quirks. "Don't you mean Mr. Brady?"

I place one hand against his firm chest, and gave him a playful shove. "Behave."

"I'll think about it," he says and I chuckle, letting my hand drop away. "When can I see you again?" he asks, his deep voice coming out almost whisper soft.

It's disorienting being the focus of all his attention. No wonder his opponents get distracted on the ice.

I chew on my lower lip, checking on my classroom yet again. I can feel a few of them watching my exchange with the hockey stud they now obviously idolize.

"I think you just got a few new fans," I murmur, eyes swinging back over to him.

"Answer me, Elise," he says.

I swallow and look down at my shoes. "I'll um, have to check my schedule and let you know."

"You better," he says, but his tone is gentle.

"I will. But I need to go hand out some animal crackers before mutiny breaks loose."

He nods, his eyes filled with amusement as he gazes down on me. "You have fun with that."

I grin. "I always do."

CHAPTER TWENTY

Emergency Intervention

Elise

I should be paying attention to the conversation around me. I should be listening like the good friend I am, and contributing at all the right moments. Instead?

I'm hyper aware of the man seated next to me. Justin is on my right, and I can't seem to stop my eyes from drifting that way every few minutes or so. I'm aware of every breath, every tiny movement. He's doing nothing more than sitting beside me nursing a bottle of imported beer, yet I'm enthralled.

His upper lip is fuller than the lower, and I'm not sure why I've never noticed that before, but all I want to do is nibble on his gorgeous lips, and gah! It's distracting. I'm not sure what's wrong with me, but I've never felt this way before.

During the season, most of the guys seem to forget how to shave. Justin hasn't, but it does seem to become more sporadic based on the delicious five o'clock shadow dusting his defined jaw. His eyes are the color of the ocean at sunset, and when they meet mine, a jolt of awareness skates through me.

I want him tonight.

Justin looks away, glancing over at Teddy who's in the middle of a story about the rookie player named Morgan and a killer play they made last weekend. But I'm left with the warmth of his big body beside mine and his lingering scent that fills me with every happy memory and safe feeling from my adolescence. I don't hate it. Not even a little bit.

I feel his hand touch my knee under the table and I'm almost surprised when I don't jump out of my seat. A knowing smile twitches on Justin's lips. He must know the effect he has on me. The smug bastard. I want to give him a taste of his own medicine, want him to feel the same sense of reckless abandon I feel whenever he's near. This out of control feeling is new for me. It's certainly not something I experienced while dating Andy, the school teacher.

Bringing one hand beneath the cover of the table, I place my palm on his thigh and give it a firm squeeze. It's less of a warning and more of a playful taunt.

But if he's affected by my touch, it doesn't show. His expression gives nothing away. He takes a casual sip of his beer and sets it on the table in front of him, his thumb picking at the label. My hand drifts further up his thigh until I reach inappropriate territory, and wait to see if I've elicited a response from him.

His mouth pulls into a frown and his eyes cut to mine. I keep my expression neutral as I explore, locating my prize, and give it a playful squeeze.

Justin's hand grabs mine and removes it from his hardening manhood, then places it on my lap. He gives me a dark look and mouths *behave*.

I shrug, fighting off a grin.

He's right though—I've never felt this reckless or daring before. It's like I've had a sexual awakening. But apparently Justin doesn't want our friends witnessing it. I guess I can't blame him. At least Owen's not here tonight. He left about an hour ago with some puck bunny he met not even fifteen minutes before. My brother is a slut, but he's also sweet and a loyal friend, so we don't give him too much crap for it.

I take a sip of my drink and try to focus, listening as Sara recounts an awful first date she went on recently.

"It couldn't have been *that* bad," sweet, innocent Becca says. "At least you're putting yourself out there and dating."

"Oh it was *that bad*. At the end of the night he actually put my hand on his crotch and suggested that it was my job to take care of his *problem* since I was the one who created it."

Becca groans in sympathy, and Sara nods, taking a long sip of her martini.

It makes me glad I'm not out in the dating scene, at least for the time being, while Justin and I explore our chemistry, and since he and I agreed to be exclusive. Honestly if we hadn't, I don't think I could have continued with this fling. Because while I've talked a big game to Becca, and made it seem like I was invincible, and that I was incapable of getting hurt during this whole thing, the truth is, I'm just like anyone else. I have insecurities and uncertainties, and since I'm ninety-nine percent certain I could never measure up to the brazen sex-pots Justin usually attracts, it's just better this way. Not to mention safer. I like knowing that he isn't sharing his body with anyone else for however long it takes us to work this attraction out of our systems. Even if I am a bit surprised at how quickly he agreed to be exclusive. Scratch that, actually it was his idea—he was the one who suggested it.

"Penny for your thoughts?" Justin says, interrupting my runaway brain.

I press my lips together. I can't exactly admit that he was the star of my daydream, especially when several sets of eyes swing over to me from across the table.

I shrug. "Nothing. I'm just glad I'm taking a break from the dating scene after the disaster that was Andy."

Sara raises her glass and clinks it against the side of mine in solidarity. "Cheers to the single life." She grins at me.

The conversation shifts to guy-code things that I'll probably never understand. I hear Teddy raise his voice, passionately defending something Sara has no doubt called him on.

"Yeah but when a girl orders a salad on a date,"

Teddy says, leaning forward on his elbows, "and then starts making googly eyes at my steak and fries, that's where I draw the line. Just order what you want. Don't steal my food."

Sara makes a low noise of disagreement.

"You always share your fries, TK. That's like a rule," Becca corrects him.

"You are literally the worst, Teddy," Sara adds, her tone firm.

"Fine." Teddy leans back, crossing his bulky arms over his massive chest. "Let's hear your side. In fact, everyone should share. Let's hear your most insightful commentary on the opposite sex."

"What do you mean by commentary? Like advice?" Becca asks.

"Sure," Teddy agrees, grinning. "Advice."

Teddy is always down for some good-natured fun. He reminds me of Owen a little, in that Owen is always in a cheerful mood and doesn't let things get under his skin. But where my brother is lighter, with sandy brown hair and gray eyes, Teddy has dark hair and deep coffee-colored eyes that crinkle in the corner when he laughs.

"I'll start," Teddy says, taking a quick sip of his

beer. "Unspoken rule—if I make a comment to a girl and it could be interpreted in one of two ways, and one of those ways offends you, I meant it the other way."

Becca chuckles softly while Sara lightly punches Teddy in the shoulder. "You're an idiot."

He flashes her a grin.

They have an interesting friendship, that's for sure. From what I've seen, their time spent together is generally filled with biting insults and complaints about the opposite sex, yet it's clear that they're close.

"You're up, bro." Teddy motions to Justin.

For a second I wonder if Justin's going to play along. He's usually not into Teddy's games, but after a pause, he opens his mouth to speak.

"If you receive one, you better give two back," Justin says.

Sara and I both grin. She raises her glass. "Here, here. Now that's my kind of man."

Teddy rolls his eyes. "Fine Justin, since you're all about doubles, why don't you give us one more."

Once again Justin considers before he speaks,

taking his time, and I'm not certain he's going to oblige, but then he does. "Absolutely nothing is hotter than a confident girl who makes the first move." Justin looks right at me as he says this and tingles race down my spine. Is he referring to earlier when I groped him under the table? Even though he made me stop, maybe he did appreciate my initiative? I'm really not sure, but I hope to find out later.

Sara signals our server for another round, and then leans forward like she's about to let all of us in on a secret. "I've got one. Women have two types of crushes. The first? Damn he's hot, I want to bang it out with him. And the second… Damn he's everything, I want to marry him."

"Men are the exact same way," Teddy says.

Everyone goes quiet for a second and I want to look to Justin to see his reaction, but I lose my nerve and then a second later, his phone is buzzing and he's fishing it from his pocket.

"It's Owen," he announces, looking down at the screen with a puzzled expression.

"What's wrong?" I lean closer, stealing a peek at his phone.

`Sex emergency, dude. 911.`

I frown as Justin begins typing out a reply. What in the world would constitute as a sex emergency?

`No condoms?` Justin replies.

`Worse. Can you come over here?`

`Now?`

`Right fucking now.`

Justin and I exchange a curious look before his phone pings again.

`ASAP. Fucking hurry.`

My stomach turns and I start to feel worried. Justin and I make eye contact again, but he just shrugs.

"I have no idea what's going on, but maybe we should go?"

I nod just as an address appears on his screen.

Justin removes his wallet from his pocket and leaves some cash on the table, enough to cover both of our drinks plus a generous tip.

"Where are you two kids off to?" Becca asks, voice slightly suspicious. I'm sure she's thinking we're taking off to hookup. Sadly, that's not the case.

"We have to go get Owen out of some jam," I say.

Becca frowns. "Is everything okay?"

Justin looks down at his phone again and whatever he sees on the screen makes him shudder. Okay that is just weird, because I've never once in my entire life seen Justin shudder.

"It's some type of sex emergency," I whisper toward Becca.

"How exactly does one have a sex emergency?" Becca asks, loud enough for the entire table to hear.

God bless drunk Becca. The girl has absolutely zero filter.

Teddy's the one that answers. "It's Owen, the dude's inventive, what can I say?"

"Elise?" Justin asks and my gaze swings over to his. "We better go."

"Right." I nod.

I give Becca and Sara a quick hug.

"Call me later," Becca requests just before Justin and I head out.

I can tell she's curious about what's happening, but honestly so am I, in a slightly morbid kind of way, because Owen is my brother, and there's a solid chance that once I find out whatever this emergency is, I'll be scarred for life. *God, the things you do for family…*

Since we'd planned to spend the night out drinking, neither of us has a car, and we have to catch a ride over to the address Owen indicated, but it doesn't take us long to arrive since there's no real traffic this time of night.

The car rolls to a stop in front of a brick apartment building, and while it doesn't look like anything sinister, I'm suddenly even more worried than I was before.

"Is he okay? I'm kinda scared to go in there," I say in a tentative voice to Justin as we step out of the car and onto the curb.

Justin chuckles, the sound low under his breath. "He's fine. He's a fucking idiot, but he'll live."

I swallow, and nod. Then I feel Justin's hand close around mine and we start up the stairs for the third floor. It's chilly out tonight and the staircase is open to the elements, so I pull my fleece jacket tighter around my body as we trudge up the steps.

We stop in front of apartment 316 and Justin knocks twice on the door before pushing it open.

The living room is empty, just a lonely beige-colored couch facing a flat screen TV. There's a scratching post for a cat, and then an orange tabby cat appears from around the corner, eyeing us with curiosity.

This is so freaking weird.

"Justin? That you?" Owen's voice calls out from a back bedroom.

"Yeah. It's me and Elise is here too."

"Fuck." Owen curses from the other room. "She needs to wait outside."

Justin's gaze swings over to mine. "Well, you heard the man."

What are we doing here? Part of me doesn't

want to know, and the other half of me is dying to find out what my old brother has gotten himself into this time.

"Stay put, okay?" Justin says, releasing my hand with a faint squeeze.

I nod, feeling slightly terrified and slightly amused.

Justin disappears inside the bedroom and his sharp bark of laughter is immediate, followed by the sound of groaning. I hear them exchange a few words, but can't make out what's being said. That might be for the best, because I'm not sure I want to know what my big brother has gotten himself into this time.

When Justin emerges a few minutes later, Owen trails behind him, buttoning his jeans and throwing his sweatshirt on over his head.

Owen won't meet my eyes, and I have the strangest feeling that something bad happened to him. As we follow Justin to the front door, I jog to catch up to him, touching his shoulder until he turns to face me.

"What happened, Owen? Is everything okay?" I ask.

Owen's expression is more somber than I've ever seen it. "I feel violated."

Justin chuckles. "Pretty sure you got what was coming to you."

"What the hell is going on?" I press again for details, but they're both moving again and I'm left with no choice but to follow.

"Let's never speak of that again," Owen says, closing the door behind us.

"Roger that," Justin agrees as we begin descending the stairs.

CHAPTER TWENTY-ONE

First Times

Elise

Do you have a waffle maker?

I stare down at the text from Justin and frown. Is this some sort of strange sexual innuendo that I'm not familiar with? It wouldn't surprise me. I'm not exactly hip on all the lingo. I recall a conversation with Sara and Bailey once where my horizons were broadened to say the least. Who knew there were so many euphemisms for lady parts? *Pink taco. Fur burger. Muff. Bearded Clam. The Notorious V. A. G., Red Wagon.* Sheesh, that was a hilarious night. Pushing the thoughts away, I shake my head and begin to compose my response.

I don't think so.

Okay. No problem. See you in 15.

Maybe it wasn't sexual after all. Maybe he's just craving waffles and I'm reading way too much into everything. Either way, I have fifteen minutes to ready myself until he arrives, and since it's not enough time to take a leisurely bath like I wanted to, I pile my hair into a bun, and take the world's fastest shower, still managing to wash and shave all the important parts somehow in under eight minutes. I've dressed in black leggings and a cream-colored t-shirt when my intercom buzzes.

He's here.

I pull my hair out of its bun and shake it out around my shoulders so my waves fall back into place.

It's been a long week of work for me and brutal practices for him, and now it's Friday evening and I have Justin all to myself until tomorrow. I'm practically giddy at the idea of that.

When I answer the door, he's already smiling. All six foot two of him is happy and excited to see me, and just that secret knowledge does something to me.

"Hey, gorgeous." His arms are filled with grocery bags, and I'm immediately suspicious.

"Hey. What's all this?" I open the door wider and he steps inside.

"Just a few things I picked up." He carries the bags into the kitchen where he begins unloading their contents onto the counters. It's then that I notice a duffel bag is strapped around his chest.

I chuckle at the thought of him packing an overnight bag. Surely he didn't bring pajamas, did he?

Across my counters are various items, bottles of champagne and red wine, a carton of chocolate covered strawberries and two dozen of the biggest pale pink roses I've ever seen.

"What in the world?" I ask, grinning.

"I didn't know if you liked champagne. I couldn't remember. So I got your favorite red too."

The label indicates it's a bottle of red wine that I rarely splurge on—generally only when Owen is buying because it's forty-five dollars a bottle. And while it tastes so much better than the ten dollar bottles I usually buy, it's a bit outside of my preschool teacher's salary.

"I like champagne. For special occasions." My voice has gone soft, and apparently Justin notices. *Is this a special occasion?* I wonder.

His smile fades away into a more predatory look and he moves across the kitchen until we're standing face-to-face. He places one hand on my waist, lightly squeezing.

Oh. Am I the special occasion?

"But the roses, the chocolate?" I ask, tilting my head in confusion. We've already had a re-do on our first time. Haven't we? Although it wasn't exactly like careful planning went into it—we just kind of fell in to bed together, our bodies desperate for contact.

He's quiet for a moment as he takes me in. There's a look of silent admiration in his eyes. "I wanted to make up for my behavior our first time together. I, um," He rubs one hand over the back of his neck, looking unsure for just a moment. "I didn't know for certain it was your first time until after, and I think your first time should be special, right?"

"What are you saying?" I cock my head, studying him.

"I want to make tonight special. For you."

My heart squeezes painfully in my chest. He wants to completely re-do our first time together. It's the sweetest, kindest thing anyone's ever done for me, but I can't let myself read too much into it.

He fucked up—he's trying to fix that—end of story.

This isn't some grand, romantic gesture, and I can't make it out to be.

"You didn't have to do all that," I say, though my smiles conveys how much I appreciate it.

There's also a bag of nacho flavored chips and a bottle of blue Gatorade. "And this?" I ask with a chuckle.

He grins, removing the duffle bag from over his head and setting it on a nearby dining chair. "Post-sex snack," he says like that makes perfect sense. "A man needs his replenishment, Elise."

"Right." I nod, feigning a serious expression. "Of course."

"Let's have a glass of champagne," he suggests. "It's already chilled."

"Perfect."

He gets to work on the cork while I locate two suitable glasses in the cabinet. I don't have champagne flutes, so my stemless wineglasses will have to do.

While he fills each one with the bubbly golden liquid, I place the roses in a vase of water and sample one of the strawberries.

"Oh my God, so good," I say, bringing one to his lips so he can taste a bite.

He makes a small, pleased sound as he chews. Then we carry our glasses to the couch and settle in side by side.

"This is so nice. We have all night," he says, bringing his glass to mine before taking a sip.

I do the same and the bubbles dance across my tongue as I swallow.

It's crisp and refreshing and delicious. I don't even want to think about how much this bottle cost. It feels so decadent to me, but maybe this isn't that big of a splurge to him at all. I often forget that Justin is a millionaire. Mostly because he doesn't act like it.

I take another sip and try to relax.

"What else did you bring?" I recall that he hadn't unpacked the last bag of groceries—or the duffel bag.

"I brought pancake mix for the morning, maple syrup, a skillet and a ladle. I wasn't sure if you had those."

I grin at him. "You thought of everything, didn't you?"

I wonder if he's also so thoughtful with all his dates, and suddenly I feel a hot pang of envy at all the women who've come before me.

I take another sip of my champagne while Justin watches me. I feel so warm and excited already, but clearly I suck at making the first move, because rather than do anything about it, I sit here, drinking my champagne while my heart flutters wildly and I grow more and more impatient.

Finally, he moves closer on the couch, setting his glass down on the table, and then removing mine from my hands to place it beside his.

He offers me his hand and when I accept, he pulls me up and into his lap so I'm straddling him.

"I really was serious about us being exclusive, Elise. For however long this lasts," he says.

I nod and press my lips to his.

We kiss deeply, our tongues moving together in an unhurried pace as I push my hips into his lap.

"God, I've missed you," he murmurs, his lips

moving to my throat. I move against him, loving the firm feel of his body beneath mine. "I want you."

"So have me," I whisper back.

Justin stands, still holding me and carries me to my bedroom. But he stops at the threshold and sets my feet on the floor. "Shit. I almost forgot. Wait here?"

I nod, unsure about what's happening.

He grabs the duffle bag from the nearby chair and shuffles past me into my bedroom. I hear him moving around the room, but it's dark and I don't have a view of what's he's doing.

I hear him stub his toe against the bedframe— I know because I've done the same thing many times—and he curses loudly. I barely hold in a chuckle.

"Justin?"

"Just one second," he calls.

What is he up to?

When Justin emerges to meet me in the hall-way, I expect his face to hold a playful grin like I've come to expect from him. Instead his expression is serious. I'm not sure what to make of that.

He lifts my hand, presses a kiss to the backs of my knuckles, and urges me to follow him. We walk the few steps into my bedroom, and I'm taken aback by the scene before me.

There are about a dozen lit tea light candles placed on every surface—a few on my nightstand, several on my dresser. The entire room has a pretty, golden glow.

There are more pink roses than I originally saw. Their long stems decorate my bedside table and a generous heaping of soft petals are scattered in the center of my bed. *Oh my God. They're in the shape of a heart.* It's so cheesy, but so perfect, I want to laugh and melt all at the same time.

I had no idea this playboy had a romantic bone in his big, overly-muscular body.

It takes me a minute to realize soft music is playing in the background—the sound is coming from his phone. I recognize the sensual, moody playlist from our time before and grin.

"Justin," my voice breaks. "This is…"

I don't get to finish that sentence because his mouth is suddenly pressing into the back of my neck in a damp kiss as he lifts my hair over one shoulder.

"You in these goddamn leggings." His firm hands skim down over my hips. "It drives me fucking crazy."

I swallow and lean into him so my back is against the wide expanse of his solid chest.

"That night you came over and cooked for us, I couldn't keep my eyes off your curves."

I love hearing his words, love getting exposure to his inner thoughts like this.

"I was half-hard the entire night." I melt back into his touch, but he's not done. Wrapping both arms around me, he rests his chin on my shoulder. "Loved having you in my space, cooking for me, feeding me, even if I couldn't show it."

I grin wryly. Hockey players can eat more than anyone. Of course the way to his affections is through his stomach. Something about that amuses me.

I have so many things I want to say. I want to thank him for making tonight so special, for all the effort he's obviously put in, but Justin turns me in his arms and leads me to the bed. I lower myself to the mattress, sitting on the edge of it. My shirt comes off and then my bra. His hands are on my breasts, already massaging and caressing as I unbutton his pants, and work my hand inside his boxer briefs. He's already hard for me and oh my fuck, that does something for me.

He makes a low groan and then leans down to pull my leggings down my hips. I lift my behind off the bed as he tugs my pants and everything down at once until he removes them completely. I'm suddenly naked while he's still fully clothed.

"No fair." I pout.

He frowns. "Are you cold? I should have turned up the heat."

I shake my head. "I'm fine. I just think you should join me." I work my hands under his shirt and press my hands to his firm stomach. His muscles jump under my touch.

Then he's pulling the shirt off over his head and dropping his pants just as quickly.

Justin Brady naked is a fine work of art, but I barely get a second to appreciate the view before he's guiding me back onto the bed. He cages me in underneath him, his forearms on either side of my shoulders as his warm body covers mine. The feeling is amazing. His hard length is pressed right over my pubic bone, and when I wrap my legs around him, it comes perfectly in line with my center.

His mouth covers mine in a hungry kiss—and we stay like that for a long time. His tongue stroking and flirting with mine while his erection grinds against me in the most maddening way possible. I've never been kissed like this. Open-mouthed, demanding, and insanely passionate.

Something that he said when we had our exclusivity talk has stuck with me.

I take a break from kissing him and touch the rough stubble on his cheek. "I want you to fuck me without a condom."

He pulls back to meet my eyes and his expression is like I've just asked him to solve a complicated mathematical equation. "What are you … talking about?"

"You're clean. I'm definitely clean. I want to feel you—for real—without a layer of latex in between us."

His eyebrows pinch together and his expression looks pained. "Fuck, Elise," he curses low under his breath. "You have no idea how badly I would *love* to do that with you, but we can't."

I chew on my lower lip as I meet his eyes. "Why not?"

"Because, for one thing I could get you pregnant."

Oh. *Right.* It's weird that the possibility of that doesn't scare the pants off of me—well, my pants are already off, but still. I shake my head. "I'm on birth control. Plus, you could pull out if you want a little back up."

I see a moment of hesitation. He wants to give in, but he's fighting with himself. "I've never done that before."

"You've never slept with someone without a condom?"

He shakes his head.

I grin. "Good. That means I get to have one of your firsts too."

At this, he chuckles, looking uncertain. "You might not realize it, but you do already own a lot of my firsts."

I make a skeptical sound in the back of my throat.

"It's true," he continues, brushing a strand of

hair back from my face as he gazes down at me.

It should feel weird to be having an entire lengthy discussion while we're both naked and aroused, and yet with him, it feels like the most natural thing in the world to be hammering out these details. It must be because I'm so comfortable with him, but regardless, I like it. A lot. I like all of the communication and quiet admissions of truth. And as eager as I am for what comes next, part of me wants to keep the conversation going.

"Remember when you and Owen went to prom?" I grin at the memory of them primping themselves in front of Owen's bedroom mirror.

"Yeah, you were in middle school, right?"

I nod. "I had such a crush on you back then. Seeing you in a tux." I grin. "It was the first time I felt like my little heart might just explode from sheer longing."

He chuckles softly, giving my shoulder a squeeze. "E-Class, I'm shocked." His mouth tilts in a wry grin. "Well I have something to admit too. I've never packed a duffle bag full of candles, or put rose petals all over someone's bed before."

My heart is so full of him, and my body is so ready for more, and I know the time for talking is done. "Then give me one more first," I whisper, bringing one hand between us. Wrapping my hand around his thick length, I guide him to my opening. Then I watch as his teeth sink into his lower lip and a sexy look of concentration flashes across his features as I start to push him inside. He tilts his hips forward, giving me what I want at an agonizingly slow pace.

A tiny pinch as I accommodate to his size and then pleasure. *So. Much. Pleasure.*

I groan and his eyes sink closed as he thrusts the rest of the way home.

"*Oh, fuck, Elise.*" His voice is broken and gruff, it's unexpectedly sexy to hear him losing control.

The warm ambience of the candlelight is surprisingly sweet, and I love it. I love being able to see him and watch his expression change as he gazes down on me. He fights off a shiver, and makes a desperate, needy noise as his lips meet mine.

His strokes grow faster, his hips snapping into mine as my volume increases.

"Yes. Like that. *Yes*," I moan.

Supporting his weight over me with one hand, he brings the other between us to apply gentle pressure.

I start to come immediately, writhing and whimpering and tightening my thighs around his trim hips as he continues to rock into me.

"Oh fuck, you're so tight. Without the condom. Jesus, I just can't…" he moans, his forehead dropping against mine. Our lips brush but we don't kiss.

I know he's close and I expect him to pull out.

But then his strong arms tighten around me as he makes a pleasure-filled sound, pumping into me in short, uncoordinated strokes as he fills me with his warmth.

He presses a long kiss to my lips, and then carefully withdraws. I curl my knees up to my chest, still panting.

"Are you okay?" He looks down at me in admiration.

I did little more than lay here, but I'm glad he looks pleased. Actually he looks more than pleased. I'm not sure I've ever seen him look this happy and tender. He touches his lips to mine again, and then runs his thumb over my core in the most distracting figure-eight.

"I got you all messy." His tone is almost reverent.

I can't help the giggle that bursts from my lips. "Trust me it was more than worth it."

Justin helps clean me up and we lay together in bed for a long time, just talking. We have sex once more, and it's slower and more drawn out, but just as hot. And then I dress in pajamas while he puts his boxers back on. We head to the kitchen, because apparently he wasn't kidding about needing a post-sex snack. We eat nacho cheese tortilla chips and drink champagne and blue Gatorade and watch bad reality TV, and it's one of the best nights of my entire life.

CHAPTER TWENTY-TWO

Pancakes and Chill

Justin

When I wake in the morning, it's to the feel of a warm palm rubbing light circles over my chest.

Elise is already awake and when I open my eyes, she smiles up at me shyly. "'Hi." Her voice is soft, just above a whisper.

"Morning." I grin at her. "How long have you been awake?"

She laughs. "Sorry, just a couple of minutes. I promise I'm not a creepy stalker watching you sleep."

I smooth her hair back from her face. "Didn't think you were."

Stretching one arm leisurely over my head, I bring it around Elise. It feels so nice to wake up here, to be warm and affectionate with each other without having to rush off or steal moments when no one's looking.

Lightly touching her skin, I turn her chin toward mine and give her a soft kiss. Elise sighs and leans into me, kissing me back.

I roll over and pull her up on top of me. She sits up, her legs on either side of my waist. I realize I'm still naked. I can feel the warmth of her through the cotton boxer shorts she wore to bed. She's so tempting, and I barely resist the urge to rock my hips up, creating the magic of friction between us. I want to push her little shorts aside and sink into her slowly, but then my brain snaps on, and I recall the previous time I woke up in her bed when Elise had turned me down after I'd suggested morning sex because she was too sore, and so the last thing I want to do is pressure her when she's not ready. Even if it was strange being told no for the first time in a decade. I need to behave. At least for now.

"I had fun last night," I murmur, lifting up on my elbows to bring my lips to hers. She meets me halfway and gives me one last gentle kiss.

"Me too."

I still can't believe that she'd wanted to have sex without a condom. Everything about last night was perfect, and making it special for her with flowers and candles and champagne eased some of the guilt I still feel about our real first time.

I heft myself up and rise to standing while holding Elise. She makes a little squeal as I place her carefully down on her feet.

"Let's make pancakes," I suggest.

She rewards me with a grateful look. "Sounds perfect." She's smiling as she quickly dresses, adding a pair of yoga pants over her tiny shorts and t-shirt ensemble.

In the kitchen, Elise starts the coffee while I mix the pancake batter and get the skillet heating.

I absolutely love this domestic, chill thing we have between us. And as amazing as the physical stuff between us is, I'm also really glad we rekindled our friendship after all that went down last year. Hearing her admit her crush on me while we laid in bed was one of my favorite moments from last night. I mean, I kind of suspected it, she didn't exactly hide it very well, but watching her lips tilt up in a grin as she remembered was so damn cute.

Elise and Owen are the closest thing I have to

family, and they're both amazing friends. Even if I hate the thought of lying to Owen right now, for now, this is how it has to be.

CHAPTER TWENTY-THREE

So Much for Casual

Elise

There's nothing quite like coming home from a long day of work and changing into your pajamas. I'm not sure why it feels so good, it just does. Maybe it's because I had the longest day ever with my usual classes and then parent-teacher conferences after, or maybe because I have cramps, but either way, I am cozy and comfortable and I give exactly zero fucks that it's only seven p.m. and I'm in my pjs. I haven't seen Justin in a week, ever since our amazing weekend together, and while I'm getting a bit antsy, I decide a night in by myself will be a good thing.

Pulling up the restaurant delivery app on my phone, I peruse my options for dinner.

Justin was planning to come over tonight, but I texted him before I left school that something had come up and I was no longer able to hang out. Thankfully he didn't ask why, and I didn't have to divulge that it was because of the volcano of blood erupting between my legs that visits every month. I'm pretty sure there's a rule against sharing such private information with your fuck buddy. Your boyfriend? No problem, you can gross him out with all the gory details and use it to your advantage to have him bring you chocolate, or ice cream, or even chop suey. But your hookup? No, he didn't need such private information. I don't want to scare the poor guy away. I'm enjoying our time way too much for that.

I've done a good job so far of keeping my emotional distance from him, and this is just one more example of how calm and in control I am. Even Becca has been impressed that I've managed to keep things so casual between us.

I place an order for Japanese—my favorite veggie roll and hot and sour soup, and then grab the remote. I turn on my show, but my mind is still focused elsewhere.

Last week I'd made dinner for Owen and Justin and it had felt like such naughty, delicious fun hiding my secret affair from my brother. I've never kept a secret from Owen, especially not one this gigantic. And I know this isn't going to last forever, and I'm determined to have fun with it while I can. I know that eventually this thing between us will fizzle out and I'll go back to being just friends with Justin, and that I'll have to be okay with seeing him with other girls. But it's not something I'm ready to think about just yet.

The memories of our sleepover, of the sex and the pancakes … it was literally perfect.

My phone chimes from the coffee table, but it's way too soon for my delivery order to be here. When I grab it, I see a text from Justin.

```
Are you sure you can't hang out
tonight?
```

I smile and type out my reply.

```
I'm sure. You can make it one
night without me, can't you, big
                        boy? ;)
```

It's meant to be playful, but as soon as I've sent the message, realization strikes and a pit settles low in my stomach. We haven't slept together in over a week. Between his travel schedule and my life, it hasn't always been easy to find the time. And if there's one thing I know about Justin, he's used to getting it on the regular. I know he said we're exclusive, but honestly the man has never had to wait around for sex. He probably hasn't been told no since the moment he was first drafted. For a second I worry that he's going to get bored with me and want to move on. But then my phone chirps again.

> I've been jacking it every night to thoughts of you. I feel like a fucking teenager again.

Even if my vagina is out of commission tonight, arousal stirs in my veins.

> That's a nice visual.

I'm about to type more to him, to keep the flirting going when I get a text message from Becca.

> What are you up to tonight? Want to grab dinner? I'm not far from your place.

I grin at her message, then type:

If I hadn't just ordered food, maybe. But I have cramps and just want to lay in bed and watch bad TV.

She sends back: That sounds amazing. You have fun with that.

While I wait for my food to arrive, I distract myself with my phone, texting Becca occasionally and scrolling through my social media feed.

I glance down and see a new text on my phone.

I'm at the store. You need anything?

Becca is a life saver.

Yes, actually I need tampons.

As soon as I click send, the horror of what I've just done sets in and my mouth drops open. I just texted that to Justin—not Becca. He wrote that he's at the store. I mixed up their threads. Oh dear God. *What have I done?* I feel like a freaking idiot for sending that to him.

He replies a second later.

```
...Okay? You need me to? I can ...
```

My eyes widen. "No, no, no, no!" I shout at the phone.

```
Omg. Sorry, no. I thought I was
writing to Becca. Please ignore
                              me.
```

He doesn't honestly think I would expect him to bring me feminine products, does he? I pray to God he just lets this drop, but something tells me he's not going to.

```
Well now I'm in the aisle, so
you might as well tell me what
you need. I wanna get the right
kind. There's a fuckton of op-
tions.
```

It's official, I'm now mortified. Beyond mortified. I actually don't need tampons anymore because I've just died. This hulk of a man, a pro athlete no less, is standing in the tampon aisle determined to make sure he 'gets the right kind.' This is *not* what's meant by friends with benefits. Someone's going to see him and he's going to be all over social media at any moment. What. Have. I. Done?

```
Don't worry about it. I really
didn't mean to send that to you.
```

His reply comes in almost immediately.

```
Consider me worried. This is
your vagina we're talking about.
I need it in tip top shape, ready
for me in a few days. Now tell
me what to get you.
```

A half-smile lifts my mouth as I shake my head. His logic is flawed, even if it's adorable. I want to tell him to forget it, but this is Justin and I have a feeling I won't win this argument.

```
Just a box of tampons please,
                    the blue box.
```

I click send and settle back on the couch, tugging the throw blanket over my lap.

```
Okay and what are we talking for
```

flow level? There's light, regular and mega.

I hope for your sake it's not mega.

I chuckle as I read his message and shake my head as my thumbs get to work composing my reply.

Regular.

I cannot fucking believe I'm having this conversation with him. A huge part of me is mortified, and the other part is completely amused, my stomach turning somersaults with each new message.

How do you feel about applicators — yes or no?

Oh dear God. My face heats up and I want to strangle him through the phone. Why is he making this so difficult?

Doesn't matter, I write back.

Applicator is fine.

Applicator it is. (Though I don't know what that means for the record), he sends back.

I picture him, this big, brawny man standing in the feminine care aisle, perusing over every box and label with care. Why does my heart melt a little at that visual?

Now let's talk scents.

My eyes widen and I bark out a laugh. He's insane. He's certifiably insane.

Just get anything. Seriously, just grab it and get out of there.

Hush. I'm doing this right. Now, what would you like your love muffin to smell like? The options are: lavender hibiscus, fresh cotton, or tropical citrus.

My love muffin? Is that what he calls it?

JUST PICK SOMETHING AND GET OUT
                    OF THE DAMN STORE.

Roger that.

I'm still reeling from our text conversation when my food is delivered. I set it on the counter and retrieve a plate, but I'm distracted.

I definitely feel a little strange about that whole text exchange, but honestly? Not *that* strange, because it's Justin, and I've never hidden anything from him. We've been friends for so long, and he just gets me. He understands my relationship with my brother, he gets my love-hate relationship with hockey. He accepts my love of fast food tacos and my obsession with watching nature shows. We watched an entire episode the other night while on the phone—him in his bed, me in mine. It was about how polar bears hunt and catch beluga whales in openings in the ice. Seriously, it was so good.

But best of all, he understands my need to explore this thing between us. That's a win-win in my book.

Only now … things are changing. I can't even pinpoint what, it's just I know that something has shifted.

A buzzing of my intercom interrupts my thoughts. Justin is here, and I leave my food on the counter to answer it. If I hadn't known him for twenty years, I'd probably be a little embarrassed to be seen like I am—dressed in a pair of baggy gray sweatpants and t-shirt with my hair up in a messy bun—but I'm sure he's seen me look worse than this, so I'm not going to stress over it. Plus, he's not my boyfriend, so it's not like I have to work to impress him. Another perk to just being fuck buddies.

I pull open my door and almost swoon at the sight of him. He looks like he's just come from the gym, dressed in a pair of black athletic joggers, sneakers, and a sweatshirt with the sleeves pushed up to reveal his thick forearms.

His mouth lifts in a wry smile as he holds up a shopping bag. "Mi'lady."

I chuckle at him, and accept the bag. "You did not have to do that. But thank you."

"It was nothing." He grins at me and leans a little closer, and I'm not sure if he wants to kiss me. "I also bought you chocolate, because I read somewhere that women crave chocolate when they're on their period."

"Oh." I swallow, completely at a loss for words. "Thank you."

"No problem." He grins at me. "Can I ask you something?"

I nod.

"Was your ... *condition* ... the reason you didn't want to hang out tonight?"

I smirk at him. "My *condition*? It's not a disease, you know."

His eyes meet mine, softening. "I know that."

"And yeah. I mean, I figured I was out of commission and wouldn't be much use to you tonight."

Something flashes across his features and his mouth turns down. "We could have still hung out. Even if we couldn't ...you know." His eyebrows raise suggestively.

Something about this warms me. And I have no idea why it didn't occur to me that he'd want to just hang out even if sex wasn't on the table. "I – I'm not sure what to say to be honest."

"It's okay." He nods to the bag in my hands. "How'd I do?"

I pull the box out and take a peek. "You did

perfectly. Thank you for this. I owe you."

He shakes his head. "It was nothing. You don't owe me anything."

He's being so kind to me, and I suddenly feel bad that I just assumed he wouldn't want to hang out. I'm not sure why I made that assumption, I guess because we're supposed to be keeping things casual, but in this moment, this feels anything but casual. He feels like a concerned boyfriend and while it's not an unwelcome feeling, it is confusing.

"Have you eaten? I ordered sushi, we could share," I offer. We both know one sushi roll wouldn't be nearly enough food for him, but I hope it's the thought that counts.

He leans in and brings one hand to my cheek. "I have groceries in the car. Owen and I are going to cook when I get home."

His fingertips on my skin send tingles racing down my spine. "Okay."

Justin steps forward, closing the distance between us and touches his lips to mine. His kiss is soft, sweet, and suddenly I feel a little lost. A little helpless and entirely too warm.

But then he's pulling back, smiling at me sweetly. "Feel better."

I hold up the bag. "Thanks again for this."

"Anytime."

I watch him leave, and then wander back into the kitchen. My sushi, which two minutes ago looked so appetizing suddenly isn't as appealing. I fix my plate and carry it into the living room, setting it on the coffee table as I pick up my phone.

Still thrown off by the turn of events over the last half hour, I fire off a quick text to Becca as I try to figure out what this new, achy feeling in my chest is all about. It's like when he walked out that door, he took some part of me with him.

I'm so fucked.

Her reply comes right away.

What's wrong??

I muster up my courage and decide to call her. This is too complicated to get into via text message.

She answers on the first ring. "Did something

happen?"

"No." I shake my head. "Yes. Maybe. I don't know!"

"Start at the beginning. Tell me what's bothering you." Her tone is soothing and I take a deep breath, trying to clear my head.

"Justin was here. He stopped by to bring me tampons."

"Oh. That's it? That's the only reason he was there?"

"Yep," I confirm, exhaling slowly as I lean back against the couch. "I'm so fucked, aren't I?"

"You've fallen for him," she says, tone matter-of-fact. She knows me well.

As soon as that blue box of tampons was in my hands, it was like something shifted. God, that sounds so stupid, but it's true. It suddenly made this entire fling into something more, something *real*. I realize now I had been lying to myself when I said that I'd be fine when this ended. Fine is the exact opposite of what I'd be. Shattered? Yes. Broken? Uh-huh. I realize now that I love him. I always have.

"Yeah," I whisper, voice shaky. "I'm in love

with him, Bec."

"Oh, honey," Becca sighs.

We both know Justin isn't capable of love and monogamy and commitment. He's the kind of guy you have a one-night stand with and then brag to your friends about the next day. I've always known that, and it's the reason I tried so hard to keep my emotions out of this and just let my body have its way. But apparently I'm not built for casual sex. I have no idea why I thought I was.

"What are you going to do now? Are you going to stop seeing him?" she asks.

"I don't know," I say, but the truth is, I do know. I just have to work up the courage to actually do it.

CHAPTER TWENTY-FOUR

Without Lube

Justin

I bought her fucking tampons? What the hell has happened to me? Last season I was playing the field, perfectly happy to fuck any woman with a nice set of tits and a mild appreciation for hockey, and now all I want is the one woman I can't have.

I have no idea when this happened, or when she started to become my whole world, but something has shifted. Elise is all I think about. When I'm on the ice—it's her I'm skating for. When I'm home in Seattle, she's the person I want to spend all my free time with. When I'm travelling, my brain is constantly calculating the difference in our time zones and when I might get to talk with her. I hardly recognize the man I've become.

I'm officially fucked.

Up the ass, as Asher would say.

Without lube, Teddy would probably add.

And Owen—well, I can't even let myself think about what Owen might say. I have a pretty good idea how he'd feel about me dating his sister and let's just say, the conversation would end with his knuckles bloody and my nose broken. It's not a road I want to venture down with him.

"You ready for this?" Owen asks from across the basketball court.

I nod and hold up both hands. He tosses me a ball as the rest of the guys file out onto the half-sized court. It suddenly seems even smaller with six huge hockey players stretching, talking trash and vying for position. The new team owner had a basketball court added to the training facility's gym last year and we've made good use of it, meeting up for quick scrimmages between game days as a way to keep our minds off hockey and stay relaxed.

We divide up into teams—me, Owen and Grant against Teddy, Asher and our backup goalie, Morgan. As the game begins, I feel myself relax, dribbling, passing and shooting. There's something about playing a sport, besides the one I'm paid to perform at the top of my game, that calms me. It must be the same for the other guys, because we all fall into an easy rhythm.

"I'm open!" Grant shouts.

Owen passes him the ball. Our captain shoots and misses, but I get the rebound.

We play until we're sweaty and tired, and then shuffle to the benches at the sidelines to grab water and towel off.

I sit down on the floor to stretch, only slightly out of breath and Owen joins me.

"You up for going out tonight?" Teddy asks Owen as he sinks down beside us.

I used to go out with them any chance I got—and now it all seems so unappealing to me—trolling bars, looking for hookups whose names I won't remember in the morning.

Owen rolls his shoulders. "Nah. Not tonight. I told Elise I was going to come to her school thingy tonight."

"What school thing?" I ask, making sure to keep my voice casual. Elise has already told me about the event, but I can't let Owen know that I know.

I move onto a hamstring stretch while Owen fills us in. "They frame and sell some of her pre-schoolers' artwork and the proceeds go to charity. I'm going to stop in and buy some shit, and then take her to dinner after."

Teddy wipes the sweat from his brow with the hem of his t-shirt. "She's not still broken up over that guy, is she?"

Owen shakes his head. "She's cool."

"Has she talked about dating again?" I ask. Teddy's already opened the door—I might as well step through it.

"Not really." Owen gives me a critical look. "Which is fine with me. Elise is the type to fall in love once and stay with the dude forever. She doesn't need to get serious about someone yet. She should just take her time. Ya know?"

As I weigh his words, an uneasy feeling settles inside me.

"I've gotta go. I've got a massage appointment in an hour," Teddy says, standing.

I nod. "Have fun with Thor."

He flips me off. Thor is the nickname we've af-fectionately given the Incredible-Hulk-sized team massage therapist. He's from Sweden and he's at least six foot six. Sports massage is often uncomfortable, especially when you have bruises and old injuries, but with him, it can be a whole new kind of torture. And all of us are pretty damn sure he enjoys inflicting that pain on us a bit too much.

Owen gets up too and starts to grab his stuff—a sweatshirt, a duffle bag, a water bottle. And every second that passes, a knot tightens in my stomach. He's heading out, planning to shower at home while I head into the gym and finish the workout I was halfway through when the guys arrived for the game.

"Hey, can I talk to you?" I jog up and stop beside him.

Even if it's the last thing I want to do, I decide this is exactly the conversation I should be having with Owen. I need to grow the fuck up and just talk to him—man to man. We've been friends for too long, and I hate the thought that there's a secret between us. Maybe there's a way to make it so everything doesn't fall apart. A knot forms in the pit of my stomach as I wait for him to respond.

Owen gives me a curious look. "Sure. About what?"

"Elise," I say, mouth suddenly dry.

"What's up?"

"That stuff you said about her not dating…"

His eyes narrow. "What about it?"

I shrug, trying to act casual while my heart-rate accelerates. This is it. This is my moment. No backing down now. *Just fucking spit it out, Brady.* "What if I wanted to date her?"

His eyes are narrowed on mine, and the grip he has on his water bottle is making his knuckles turn white. A shocked expression crosses his face, eyes widening. "You? You don't date, you fuck around, so no. I'm not giving you my blessing to fuck my sister over." His shakes his head, as if clearing away the thought of it, as if it's the most absurd thing he's ever heard.

We stand there a moment longer, him, looking at me like I've suddenly grown two heads.

"Yeah, well maybe that's all behind me. Maybe I'm ready for a good girl. There's no one better than Elise, you said so yourself."

He shakes his head again, lips pressing into a line. "Don't make me kick your ass, Brady. You know my sister is off-limits."

"I know she's your sister, but seriously, Owen, think about it. She's going to start dating again at some point."

"Is this your idea of a joke? I don't know what the fuck is wrong with you," Owen says, gaze narrowed.

I know something was wrong with me. I just can't tell my best friend what it is.

He's right though. Something inside me had changed. Ever since I thought I had a kid on the way, all the locker room talk has gone stale. This entire lifestyle has grown stale. Actually, that's a lie. I still love playing hockey, and hope to continue doing so professionally for at least another ten years if I can. Hell, maybe I'd even coach after that. What I had grown tired of was the constant female attention and meaningless sex. And before you revoke my man card—first let me explain.

As good as the release of endorphins felt, as nice as physical pleasure was, there was something about it that bothered me immensely. It was the fact that the ladies who threw themselves at the players on my team would have been just as happy to land in any of our beds.

I wasn't special. I just happened to wear a jersey that afforded me a lot of attention.

"Brady?" he asks, interrupting my thoughts. "What the fuck, man?"

I shrug, trying to keep my tone casual. "Not a joke. I just wondered how you'd feel if I asked her out."

The vein in his neck throbs and he looks like he wants to hit something. That something most likely being me.

He might think this conversation was coming out of left field, but lately, more and more, I wanted something, *someone* that was just for me. I knew it was kinda fucking weird coming from the guy who's been the king of hookups for the better part of the last decade. I'm not going to hide from the fact that I've had a lot of sex. That's part of my history. And plus, I'm holding out hope that the girl I end up with might appreciate the fact that I know what I'm doing in bed.

I still wasn't sure that girl would be Elise. Partly because I knew she was too good for me, and partly because I recognized that my friendship with her brother was going to be an obstacle. Still, I had to hold onto some hope, because I'd never felt about anyone the way I feel about her.

Owen releases a slow, strained sigh. "First, you and I both know there's not a chance in hell you're actually interested in Elise, or any good girl for that matter, because you've said time and time again you're never going to get married or have a family because of how fucked up your parents' marriage was."

I swallow a lump the size of a hockey puck. "Right. I know. I just, never mind."

"Second," he continues. "It would complicate the fuck out of things between us. Is that really something you want to risk?"

I clench my hands into fists at my sides, and nod. "No, and you're right. I get it. I really do."

Owen scoffs, muttering something under his breath as he strolls away.

Well that went fucking horribly.

CHAPTER TWENTY-FIVE
Messy, Inconvenient Feelings

Elise

"**M**ost guys suck at oral," Sara says, running a finger along her frosty pint glass. "That's just a fact of life."

"Bull-shit," Teddy scoffs, drawing out the word in lazy disbelief.

Becca chuckles quietly from the other side of the table. Justin and Owen are here too.

We're all out for a drink after the game—unfortunately the guys lost this one three to one—and were outplayed from the start. Even my normally cheerful brother is a little more somber than usual. Though I have a feeling the alcohol and Sara's taunting stories will help get their mind off the loss.

"I happen to know for a fact that I'm amazing with my tongue," Owen says, smirking into his glass.

"Gross." I roll my eyes at him. Let's file that under *Stuff I Do Not Want to Know About My Brother.*

He shrugs. "What? I've never had an unhappy customer."

Sara leans forward, placing her elbows on the table. "And that's just it, you jackass, girls won't tell you that you suck. They don't want to damage your *fragile ego*." She makes air-quotes as she says this. "They'd rather fake an orgasm to get you to stop tongue-lashing their lady bits than set you straight."

I chuckle into my wineglass. When Sara's on a roll—look out. And tonight she's in rare form. God, I love her.

"Is that true?" Owen asks, looking to Becca with a slight panic in his eyes.

I know what he's thinking—the fact that they're close means she wouldn't lie to him, but the thing is, I doubt she's in much of a position to offer an opinion. Becca's lack of sex life has been a frequent conversation of ours. I never thought much of it—I thought she was just being choosy—but lately I'm starting to wonder if there's more to it, and if it's related to the sexual assault that she swears she's past.

Owen seems to realize his mistake as Becca shrugs, her wide blue eyes on his reminiscent of a deer caught in headlights.

Sara and Teddy continue to debate on the finer points of what makes for good cunnilingus while the rest of us chuckle quietly.

My cheeks feel a little warm as Sara argues with my brother and Teddy.

Justin is seated across from me, right next to Owen, and I can feel his eyes on me the entire time. It's unnerving because I have no idea what he's thinking about.

Justin stays decidedly quiet during the entire debate, and I think I know exactly why that is. Unlike my brother and Teddy who rush to defend themselves, Justin doesn't need to. He knows he's good at it. Not just good, he's freaking spectacu-lar. And I know for a fact there's no way I'd even consider faking an orgasm with him. He wouldn't stand for it. He's not satisfied until I've had at least two or three. And he'd be able to tell if it wasn't the body-quaking, breath-stealing real thing.

"And what about giving head?" Teddy asks,

voice a little too loud. I'm worried the other patrons sitting nearby are getting an earful. I place my finger over my lips as I give him a pointed stare. "Why the double standard?" he asks, lowering his voice. "Don't you think it's only fair women should know what they're doing?"

Sara calmly takes a sip of her beer, thinking. She's an attorney, so I know she's going to win this debate, but part of the fun is I never know what's going to come flying out of her mouth next. "Don't kid yourself. Men are just happy to have their cock out—I could slap it around randomly and you wouldn't complain."

He swallows, his throat visibly bobbing. "Truth."

He and Owen share a fist bump across the table.

We all laugh. My eyes wander to Justin and even he has cracked a smile. He's seemed too serious tonight. I'm not sure if it's the loss to the Spartans that has him feeling down, but at least this topic has seemed to lighten everyone's mood. Sara is kind of genius like that. Well, everyone except for Becca. I suddenly feel a little guilty.

"Let's get one more round," I suggest. "And Becca can fill us all in on the latest team gossip."

She smiles warmly at me, obviously thankful for the change in topic, and my heart squeezes a little.

• • •

At the end of the night Becca and I share a ride home, Sara takes a separate Uber and the guys stay behind. I have no doubts that Owen and Teddy will seek consolation for losing the game in the arms of a willing puck bunny, but Justin is a wildcard. It's not that I think he'd hook up with anyone else, I trust his exclusivity pact, it's that I don't know if he'll try to sneak away from the guys tonight to come and see me, or opt to hang with his buddies. I'm trying not to feel disappointed either way.

After a quiet ride across town, the car drops Becca off first, and then I'm alone with my thoughts, my eyes drifting to my phone every few minutes. Although we'd texted over the past several days, Justin and I haven't been alone together since he'd delivered tampons to my front door. Maybe he thinks I'm still on my period. I decide to text him first, and pull out my phone, just as a message from him pops up.

Can I come over?

I grin as I type out my reply.

Of course.

Ten minutes later, I'm opening my front door to a somber looking Justin. He's dressed in dark jeans, boots with red laces, and a gray pullover that's been thrown on over a white t-shirt. It's obviously the same thing he's been wearing all night, only now I can gaze at him appreciatively.

"Everything okay?" I ask.

He nods. "I'm just getting tired of lying to your brother."

My stomach tightens. That makes two of us. I know we need to talk about where things are headed between us, but everything inside me is screaming not to. At least not right now. Not in this moment. I just want to enjoy tonight, and live in this tiny bubble for a little while longer before it all comes crashing down around us. I have a feeling if I open my mouth, all of my truth is going to come pouring out, and I'm not ready to go there yet. I'm not sure if I'll ever be ready.

"Come here," he says softly, drawing me to his chest. His strong arms close around me.

I step closer and lay my head against his chest. His heartbeat thumps out a steady rhythm and my own speeds up in agreement. I don't ask him to tell me what he said to Owen and the other guys to get out of there tonight, though I can tell it's weighing on him.

Two fingers under my chin lift my face toward his and then his lips touch mine. They're firm, yet soft and I melt into his touch. His scent surrounds me and I'm overcome with so much emotion, my heart squeezes almost painfully. With a soft groan, he parts my lips with his tongue, our kiss deepening immediately with hungry urgency.

I push my fingers into the hair at the back of this neck and tug him even closer. Close enough that I can feel the pulse of his steely erection between us. That does something to me, and before I can even contemplate my next action, I'm climbing him like a damn tree.

"Yes. Come here. *Fuck*," Justin groans, lifting me so I can wrap my legs around his waist, bringing us even closer together.

I can feel his excitement trapped between us, and my panties grow damp with eagerness.

With focused efficiency, Justin stalks toward

my bedroom, not letting go of me for even a second. Then I'm being placed down in the center of my bed and he hovers over me, his mouth still on mine.

"Get naked," he says, voice rough.

I'm not sure what's changed, or what happened tonight, but this is the first time he's been so demanding, or dared to issue a direct order. Normally he's so sweet, checking in and asking if I'm ready. Tonight there's a desperate gleam in his eyes and I can't help but comply. I'm out of my jeans and sweater in about four seconds and Justin does the same, stepping out of his boots to quickly rid himself of his jeans, boxers, and shirt.

I unsnap my bra as Justin draws my panties down my thighs.

"Shit," he curses. "I need to be inside you.""Yes," I murmur, body clenching wildly at the needy sound of his deep voice.

Not even ten seconds later, Justin is touching carefully between my legs, making sure I'm ready for him. A whimper tumbles from my lips, and then he positions himself at my opening—filling me— his thick cock pushing into me in gentle thrusts, as his fingers tangle in my hair and his lips brush the shell of my ear.

"So tight. So good," he groans.

"Yes. More." I'm practically incoherent, unable to speak in complete sentences, but thankfully he doesn't seem to mind.

He thrusts home, and I whimper, clinging to his muscles as he moves.

"Sweet fuck, Elise." His voice is little more than a rough growl. Chill bumps break out over the back of my neck, skating down my spine.

The pace he sets is brutal and punishing and I love every sinful second of it.

"Yes. Oh my God." I moan and bite his neck lightly. I feel his answering smile against my chin.

"Naughty girl." He groans against my neck, one hand pressing into my hip as he continues thrusting above me.

Soon, the time for talking is done because we're both chasing our own release in hearty pants and breathy moans.

He feels so perfect. So good. So right.

"You getting close?" he asks, voice tight.

"Yes!" I cry out, unable to contain my excitement.

With a barely concealed chuckle, he brings one hand between us and touches me in soft circles. It's crazy how well he knows my body—knows exactly the things to do to extract pleasure from me. And moments later, I go off like a rocket, my body spasming wildly as I climax. Without a condom, I know he can feel every pulse and flutter, and Justin isn't far behind, squeezing my backside with one hand as he buries himself deep and comes inside me with a low groan.

"Fuck. You're perfect," he says, breathless as the waves of pleasure finally begin to abate.

He presses a kiss to my lips, my cheek, my chin, my temple, and I smile. Then he slowly withdraws, carefully breaking our connection. I hate the loss of his body heat, but moments later he's back and I feel a warm, wet cloth wiping gently between my legs. I squeeze my eyes closed and fling one hand over my face while I chuckle at him.

"I can do that myself, you know?"

He shushes me with a quiet noise. "I know you can. But I'm the one who made you all messy, so let me clean you up. It's the least I can do."

I grin, unable to hide all of my feelings for this man.

I hear the toilet flush and then the water running, and then he's back in the bed with me, spooning his big body around mine. The room is almost completely dark, with just a little moonlight and some ambient light from the hallway filtering in, but it's enough. I can see bits and pieces of him as he moves under the blankets with me, arranging us both so we're comfortable. My heart is so full and happy that he's staying the night. I can't even put into words what it means to me.

We lay together, his arms around me for a long time before either of us speaks.

"I'm sorry you lost tonight," I say, finally. "You looked good on the ice if it matters."

He smiles down at me, his eyes soft. "It's alright. And coach said the same thing in the locker room."

I could get lost in his deep blue stare. And there are so many other things I want to say. The words *I love you* are right on the tip of my tongue and I wonder what the fuck is wrong with me. That's not part of the deal, and I certainly can't tell him that, no matter how badly I might want to.

"Come on. Let's get some sleep."

I nod. "Right. Sorry, I'm sure you're exhausted after the game."

He tugs me closer, his eyes sinking closed already.

I love the feeling of being held by him. I close my eyes and try to pretend nothing has to change.

It almost works.

CHAPTER TWENTY-SIX

Bruised and Battered

Justin

"**C**ome inside. He should be home any minute," I say to Elise when she shows up at our front door looking for Owen.

She grins at me and then lifts up on her toes to steal a quick kiss. I kiss her back, but then chuckle, shaking my head.

"Don't tempt me."

Elise's lips twitch with a smile and she follows me inside. "Are you sure you can't come to dinner with us?"

I shake my head. "You guys have fun. I don't want to interrupt brother-sister bonding time."

She rolls her eyes and then wanders into the living room and sinks into the oversized couch. I lower myself carefully to the cushion beside her.

Elise frowns. "What's wrong?"

I shrug. "Just some bruised ribs. I got stretched out and taped up after today's practice, but I'm still a little sore."

She makes a concerned sound, shaking her head. "Let me see."

I lift up one side of my t-shirt and Elise inhales sharply. The left side of my body is purple and blue.

"Oh, Justin. That looks so painful. Are you sure you're okay?"

I lower my shirt and release a slow breath. "I'll be fine." The truth is, I've had much worse injuries over the eight years I've been playing in the pros.

"Can I do anything? Ibuprofen? A massage? Anything?"

Considering her offer, I meet her eyes. I'm trying to decide how much trouble I'd been in if Owen came home and found her hands on me, and then I weigh if I actually care at this point. The desire to have her touch me wins out. Plus, I could really use some of these knots worked out.

"I'd love a massage." Tugging my t-shirt off

over my head, I move to the floor so I'm sitting in between her parted knees.

Elise's warm palms press into my shoulders and I release a slow breath. She kneads the over-used muscles in my back, pressing one hand flat against my spine.

"Ah…" I groan. "That feels good."

"Why didn't you say anything? I'm happy to do this anytime you want." I can hear the smile in her voice when she answers.

She continues rubbing my deltoids, moving lower to massage my arm muscles. It feels so nice.

"You know, I've been thinking," she says as she works.

"About?"

She takes a break from rubbing my back and fishes something out of her pocket, setting it on the coffee table in front of us. It's a key. "I had an ex-tra made for my apartment. I figure you can use it when you come over and then you can come and go as you please, like even if it's late, like after a game."

Something in that statement catches me off-guard. I know we're overdue for a discussion about this—about us—about everything, but I wasn't expecting it to unfold quite like this.

"I'm not sure what to say."

A key? A key is a huge fucking step. We only agreed to be friends with benefits, and now sweet, little naïve Elise wants to give me a key? A wave of worry passes over me. I know right then, without a doubt, that I hold the ability to crush her. To break her heart. It's a heavy thought and one I'm not okay with. Because the truth is, I'm not boyfriend material. Owen was right about that.

I'm nothing more than an easy fuck, the fun-time guy girls want a casual night with. I'm not really built for more. And even if it was what I wanted, the fact is she needs someone who will actually be in town more than he's gone. Someone who's emotionally available and capable of love, not someone like me.

It's in that moment I realize I'm never going to be good enough for her. I'm never going to be the kind of man she needs, and part of me doesn't even trust myself or believe I could commit to one woman, no matter how desperately I might want to. Owen was one-hundred percent right. I would only end up fucking her over.

"Justin?" She's stopped touching me, and even though I hate it, it's better this way.

Raising to my feet, I stand before her.

Her lips are turned down and she's studying me with narrowed eyes. "Say something."

What is there to say? I come from a broken home and have seen firsthand how love can turn to hate and bring out the very worst in people? Or that I don't trust myself not to fall into bed with some puck bunny a year down the road when things get hard? Plenty of guys on the team are in committed relationships, and it's never stopped them from screwing around before. Why should I be any stronger? I'll only end up hurting Elise and that's not a scenario I can live with.

"Listen," my voice comes out cold and much more detached than I feel, "this started as something fun, but taking your key? That's too much. I can't."

"Fine," she snaps, standing to face me. "Don't take the key. But why are you acting so weird right now?"

"Because you need a man who will be there for you. Someone who can come to your school functions, who can to bring you tampons, someone who doesn't have such an intense travel schedule. Someone who feels worthy of taking your key."

Planting one hand on her trim hip, Elise frowns. "I'm used to a hockey schedule. It's all I've ever known my entire life. I've never once complained about you being gone. Yes, I miss you when you're not here, but I have my own life, Justin, in case you didn't notice."

"It's more than that okay?"

Her pretty face falls. "Don't do this," she says, voice firm. "Don't do this to us…"

The front door opens and Owen strolls inside. It takes him exactly three seconds to notice the tense mood between me and his sister. *Just fucking fantastic.*

Stopping on the other side of the couch, his eyes harden as he looks between us. I'm still shirtless and Elise looks visibly upset.

"What is this?" Owen demands.

Elise sniffs, lifting her chin. "It's nothing, Owen. Just give us a minute, would you?"

He lets out a humorless laugh, coming closer. I don't miss the way his hands curl into fists at his sides. "Are you fucking kidding me? You couldn't stay away from my sister? My goddamn *sister*. Fucking prick."

"It's not like that," I say.

"Oh yeah, what's it like then? Why don't you tell me?"

My throat feels tight, but I force the words out. "I really liked her."

"Liked?" Elise scoffs. She doesn't miss my past-tense slip-up.

Fuck.

Placing one hand against my ribs, she looks up at me, those striking blue eyes cutting straight through me. "I'm not giving up on you, Justin, you have so much more to offer than you realize. But I have to go. We'll talk later."

I nod once.

Then she looks at Owen. "And in case you didn't notice, I'm an adult. So you can either fuck off and leave me alone, or you can actually be supportive like the big brother I thought you were."

Owen's gaze locks on mine and for a second I'm sure things are about to turn physical between us. But then he looks back to Elise and nods. "Let's go."

I watch them leave the apartment. Elise doesn't even bother looking back at me.

Now my ribs match how my heart feels—bruised and battered. But it's fine, because it's exactly what I deserve. And since part of me always knew it would end this way, I feel relieved that it finally did.

CHAPTER TWENTY-SEVEN

Poker Face

Justin

"**P**ass the salsa?" Becca asks in an overly sweet voice from the far end of the table.

With a sigh, I obey, picking up the bowl and carrying it down to her. We're all over at Teddy's for a poker night. It used to be a regular thing, but we haven't gotten together to play for a while now. And while it'd normally be something I looked forward to, tonight I almost hadn't come. First, because Elise is here, and we haven't spoken in three days. Not since the *key* incident, as I've started calling it. And second, I haven't been able to talk to Owen about any of this. Which sucks almost just as much. We've pretty much avoided each other, avoided any conversations more serious than *grab me a beer*, or *do you want a ride to practice*?

Everything's been turned upside down, and I know it's entirely my fault. Her trying to give me a key to her place shouldn't have freaked me out so bad, but it did. And now here we are.

"You know who else likes salsa?" Becca asks, smiling up at me hopefully. "Elise."

My lips twitch with a smile. I fell for that pretty damn fast. "I don't think she wants to talk to me right now," I say in a low voice. She'd probably rather throw this bowl of salsa in my face than have a conversation with me.

My gaze wanders toward the kitchen where Elise stands with Sara and Bailey. I can't hear what they're discussing, but man does she look beautiful. Her hair is tied back in a loose ponytail, and there's a slight blush to her cheeks.

I keep trying to tell myself that I did the right thing. She's in no place to make decisions about a future relationship. She's young. I'm the first fucking man she's been with, there's no way she could know what she wants. Christ, I've sampled all fifty-two flavors at the ice cream shop, and I'm still not sure I could tell you which one was my favorite. Actually that's a lie.

Elise.

Elise is my favorite.

And it's not because the sex is good—though it is fucking great—it's because of the way she makes me feel.

The way she looks at me.

The way she sets my skin on fire.

She's smart and funny and sweet. And my money and abilities on the ice mean absolutely nothing to her. She liked me when I was a nerdy thirteen-year-old who was awful at checkers and liked only bacon on my pizza. Though, to be fair, I still like bacon on my pizza.

Spending time together was just as enjoyable as the sex we'd been having, but I can't give more.

Besides, she's the one who laid down those ground rules that first night I took her home. She wanted a fling, and I was determined to give her exactly what she wanted, because the alternative—some douchey guy in her bed while she sowed her wild oats—was not an alternative I could live with. But I can't trust myself with her heart, and I can't trust that she's ready for commitment like she thinks she is. *Fuck, this is hard.*

"Justin?" Becca says, still looking up at me,

with a hopeful expression.

I realize I've just been standing here holding a bowl of salsa for several minutes.

I take a deep breath. "Right. Sorry."

Gripping the bowl of salsa like it's a grenade, I wander into the kitchen. Sara and Bailey see me coming before Elise does and they excuse themselves mid-sentence. With a confused expression, Elise's gaze swings over to mine.

"Oh." She parts her lips, freezing almost awkwardly, like she knows there's no polite way to escape the kitchen.

"Hey," I say softly, stopping right in front of her. "Becca said you might want some salsa."

It's a lame attempt at small talk, but fuck, I'm not good at this.

She frowns. "I'm good, thanks."

Shit.

I set the dish on the counter and meet her eyes. "I didn't come in here to offer you salsa."

"No?" she asks, voice sarcastic. "Why did you come in here then?"

I swallow my pride and take a deep breath. "Can we talk? In private?"

Elise's gaze strays over to Owen. He's playing a hand of cards and hasn't noticed us talking. For a moment I think she's going to refuse me, and I know it's what I deserve, but damn does that thought sting.

"Please," I tack on, voice soft.

"Okay," she says finally. "You have three minutes."

I'll take it. "Let's go out onto the balcony."

She nods at my suggestion and follows me to the sliding glass doors. It's cool outside, and she's not dressed for the weather. But luckily, the portico covers us from the light rain falling from the night sky.

Elise wanders over to the outdoor sofa and tests the cushion to be sure it's still dry before she takes a seat.

I sit down on the ottoman in front of her, offering a half smile. "So …."

But Elise is not amused. "If you've got something you want to say, say it."

"I fucked up." The words are out of my mouth before I can sensor myself.

"Okay. I'm listening."

"I fucked up my friendship with Owen. I fucked up my relationship with you…."

Her eyes soften as she looks at me, but she doesn't deny it.

"And the thing is, I don't even regret it."

She studies me without speaking, her eyes intent.

"That doesn't make sense…what I mean is… You know how you said you had a crush on me way back when? Well, I can't say I felt that way when you were in middle school because…gross. But later, I've been feeling something too. For years now. But I pushed it down because I knew it wouldn't be simple. It wouldn't end easy."

"Maybe it's okay that things aren't simple. Maybe it's worth the risk."

"But all the risk would be on you. I'm an escape, Elise. Not long-term boyfriend material. You know that as well as I do. I travel half the year for games and public appearances. My schedule is fucked. It would be selfish of me to expect more.

So I took what I can—and now look where it's gotten us."

"I've been happy with where it's gotten us. I even made you a key—which you spectacularly rejected, by the way."

"I don't want to throw away what we have, but I know you deserve someone better."

At this, Elise leans forward and places her hand on my arm. "There's no one better than you. Believe me, I've looked."

I know I'm not ready for this to end. But am I ready for more? That's the million-dollar question.

CHAPTER TWENTY-EIGHT

Stubborn Emotions

Elise

I'm sitting face-to-face with Justin outside on the balcony of Teddy's apartment, and even though he's the master at keeping his feelings under wraps, I think I've finally figured it out.

He's scared.

His parents didn't love him—not unconditionally, not with their whole hearts like they should have—and now, he doesn't really believe in how lovable he actually is.

But still part of me can't believe he'd just throw away what we have because he's scared. I know I should probably take my pride and walk away. But I'm just not willing to do that. I guess I'm more stubborn than I thought.

"I know this is more than we bargained for, that this is more than what we set out for this to become, but I think you're running scared right now because you feel something for me, and you don't know how to handle it."

He doesn't disagree and my God, his eyes—they are so dark and intense—I feel it all the way down in the depths of my soul.

His lips part, but before he can respond, the sound of the door opening interrupts us and when I look up, I see Owen strolling out.

"You okay?" he asks, stopping across from us.

I nod. "I'm fine. We're just talking."

Owen's gaze cuts straight through me. "About?"

"I know your opinion on things, but I care about Elise," Justin says. "I would never hurt her intentionally. I lov—" He stops himself, but my smile is huge.

Love.

Justin loves me.

Even if it scares him. Even if this is a horrible idea. Even if Owen is about to punch him and cause immeasurable pain—he loves me.

Me.

His best friend's little sister.

The girl who has admired him from afar all these years.

"I won't mess this up," he says, looking directly at me, but talking to Owen.

"We're going to have words about this," Owen says, his tone holds the edge of a warning. "The first hint of you dicking her around, I'll take you out with my bare hands." And then seconds later, he's strolling back inside.

I launch myself into Justin's arms, smiling.

I press a kiss to his scruffy cheek and can feel him smiling back against my lips. "Did you really mean all that?"

"Every word," he says, voice gruff. "I've fallen for you. So fucking hard."

My heart clenches in my chest.

"When you made me that key …"

I stop him. "It scared you."

He nods. "It did, but that's just stupid." I'm about to disagree with him, to tell him it's not stupid, but he keeps talking. "I'm done being scared. I know I might not be boyfriend material, and it's possible that I'll suck at all of this, but I want to try. For you. Because the idea of living without you in my life?"

His expression in pained. I lean in and press a soft kiss to his lips.

"You won't suck."

He smiles. And wow, it is so good to see him smile again. A knot of unease I've been carrying around inside me all week evaporates in an instant. "You sure about that?"

I pat his scruffy cheek again. "I'm positive. Unless you plan on hooking up with puck bunnies or doing something incredibly stupid like…"

I don't get to finish because he's shaking his head and scowling at me. "I would never do that to you. You're the only one I want."

Maybe it's crazy, and maybe it's completely foolish of me, but I actually believe him. I know Justin's been with enough women to know what he wants. And if he says he wants me…I believe him.

Leaning closer, I press my lips to his and Justin's fingers sink into the hair at the back of my neck, holding me close so he can deepen the kiss. His tongue sweeps against mine and heat flickers low in my belly.

"You want to go back inside and play poker?" he asks, breaking our connection, but keeping his forehead against mine.

I shake my head. "I have a better idea."

His smirk is delicious. "And what would that be?"

"You. Me. My place."

"Fuck yes," he whispers. "Let's go."

I feel almost giddy as we head inside. And almost immediately all eyes in the room whip over to us. Justin laces his fingers through mine, as if to announce to the world that we're together.

I secretly love that he's not being shy about this. I love that we're coming out as a couple to our friends. After months of hiding what happened between us and hiding my feelings, this is a very welcome change of pace.

I lean my head on his shoulder, the difference in height between us exaggerated. Justin rubs one hand along my shoulder, keeping me close. "So, we're going to … get out of here."

There are whoops and hollers and catcalls from around the room.

And then money changes hands, Asher paying Teddy with a frown. "You were right," he mutters.

"What the?" Justin asks.

Teddy shrugs. "We made a bet. It's about damn time you guys realized how perfect you are for each other."

I see Becca grinning at me from the kitchen.

"That's fucked up," Owen grumbles, obviously grossed out that his own friends took bets on his sister and best friend.

When we cross the room, Justin stops in front of Owen and shakes his hand. I'm just relived when Owen doesn't punch him. Some silent understanding passes between them and I grin at their exchange, finally feeling at peace that everything is out in the open. But then Justin is pulling me toward the front door, and a whole new wave of emotion hits me.

CHAPTER TWENTY-NINE

Ice time

Elise

"**W**hat in the world?" I smile, keeping my eyes closed just like Justin asked.

His hands on my waist lead me down a cement walkway, my heels clattering in the otherwise quiet room. Before I can ask him again where he's taking me, the smell gives it away. Hockey arenas just have a certain smell.

I grin, confused. "You brought me to the ice rink?" *What in the heck?* Did he forget that he has practice today or something?

This is all still brand new between us, and I love that he's trying. *But, huh?* It's obvious I'm clearly not used to this side of him.

He chuckles. "Open your eyes."

I do, and then for a moment, I'm speechless. When he'd wanted to practice this whole boyfriend thing, Justin insisted on planning a special date for us this weekend, and I'd been more than happy to hand over the reins. Only now, I'm totally confused. He brought me to the ice arena where he spends countless hours each week training and working… it makes no sense.

Until suddenly it does.

First, we have the entire place to ourselves. There's something about it that feels special and a tiny bit forbidden.

With a smile playing on the edges of my lips, I take a look around.

The overhead lights in the stadium are turned off, and the only light comes from the glittery disco-ball overhead. It throws tiny silver drops of light all over the ice. It almost looks magical.

Justin presses a button on his phone and all around us, low music fills the silence. He leads me over to the bench where there's a fuzzy plaid blanket, two pairs of skates and a thermos.

"We have the whole place to ourselves," he says softly, meeting my eyes.

My confusion gives way to a smile. We haven't skated together in years. We used to all the time growing up, but somewhere along the way, that stopped.

It's crazy how the chill in the air, and even the smell of the ice can spark up nostalgia. This is us. Our history. And he planned the entire thing without me knowing.

"This is amazing," I murmur, following him to the bench where I take a seat.

He pours me a mug of hot cocoa, which I sip while he kneels before me to lace up my skates.

Then he takes off his shoes and puts on his own skates while I watch, finishing my cocoa.

"Ready?" he asks, grinning mischievously at me.

"Yes, but I'm going to be a little rusty."

He offers me his hand and I take it, following him out onto the ice. He glides effortlessly along, keeping a firm hold on my hips so I don't fall.

The breeze lifts my hair and I watch him, feeling deliriously happy as we move across the ice together.

Justin leans down and steals a kiss, chuckling. "You taste like chocolate."

It's been a month since we officially started dating and came clean to my brother, and every day seems better than the last.

"This is pretty much the best date ever," I laugh, clinging to his biceps.

"I'm glad you approve. I wasn't sure if you'd like it."

I like it for so many reasons. Because it reminds me of our childhood, and because it's just so him. I like that we're not at a hoity-toity restaurant surrounded by people and pretense, and I can rest my head on his chest as he holds me.

"I love it," I say, meeting his eyes.

He touches my cheek, tucking my hair behind my shoulder as he gazes down at me. "I love you."

Emotion lodges in my throat and tears well in my eyes. It's the first time he's said those words, and a tidal wave of emotion threatens to knock me over. Being on skates doesn't help.

Justin lowers his lips to mine as we slow in the center of the ice. "Don't cry, baby."

"I love you too," I murmur, bringing my hands around his neck. Raising on tiptoes isn't possible in skates, so I urge him lower. Dipping his head toward mine, Justin captures my lips in the sweetest kiss.

CHAPTER THIRTY

Those Three Little Words

Justin

I *love you too.*

Hearing those words on Elise's lips is the sweetest sound. And not just because I know she really does love me, but because for me—someone who's spent much of his life feeling unlovable— feeling like a total fuck up—it means everything to me.

I've spent a decade working my ass off to make it in the pros, and then all my downtime partaking in all the carnal pleasures life had to offer, but none of it made me feel the way I do when I'm with her. I feel whole. For the first time in a long time. Maybe ever.

Leaning down, I place my lips against hers and

give Elise a slow, tender kiss. We skate for a little while longer, her arms wrapped around my waist to steady herself, and my chin resting on the top of her head.

"Are you getting cold?" I ask after a while.

Elise looks up at me and nods. "A little."

"Come on then. Let's go warm you up."

We finish up on the ice and I maneuver us back to the bench.

I help Elise remove her skates, and she grins, watching me the entire time.

My phone pings from beside us on the bench and I grab it, seeing my mom's name appear. When I read her text, I let out a slight groan.

Elise frowns. "What is it?"

I shake my head. "It's nothing. It's just that my mom's been asking me about my Thanksgiving plans."

Elise nods. "So … are you going to go home for the holiday?"

I've spent many holidays—Christmases, Thanksgivings, and Easter dinners with the Parrish family—always tagging along with Owen. Usually because my own parents were either fighting, or vacationing with their new significant others, or just too caught up in their own lives to think about including me. And because Elise and Owen's parents never made me feel like I was intruding. They were always nothing but welcoming, although I can't help but wonder if this year will be different now that I'm dating their daughter. God, I hope not, because they're pretty much the only family I have.

"I don't know. I haven't decided yet."

Elise knows about the complicated relationship I have with my parents, and she never judges me for it. "Maybe we should go together," she suggests.

I meet her eyes. "You would do that?"

She nods, grinning. "Of course I would." She stands and slips her feet into her shoes while I work on removing my own skates. "In fact, I think it'd be fun. We could do dinner at your mom's and then dessert with my parents."

Her eyes are alight and her cheeks are bright. I can tell what she's thinking—that it'll be our official coming out as a couple. It's not a bad idea. We're going to need to do that soon anyway. I still haven't exactly hammered things out with Owen. He's stayed out of my way, and I've tried not to parade my relationship with his sister around in front of his face. But it's all going to need to come out in the open eventually, because my days of sneaking around with her are behind me. I want everyone to know we're a couple.

"Let's do it," I say.

Elise grins, and I can't help stealing one last kiss.

"Come on. I have one more surprise to show you."

Her pretty gray eyes narrow on mine, and she nods. "I can hardly wait."

• • •

"You saved them all these years?" Elise asks, turning the homemade knit mittens over in her hands. "Why? I don't understand."

After we'd arrived home from the ice arena, I'd led her to my bedroom and sat her on the edge of the bed. Then I'd hunted through my walk-in closet until I found the box marked *Home.* I wanted to show her something I've kept with me all these years. The pair of mittens she'd knitted for me were mismatched and coming undone, but I'd loved them all the same. One was gray and blue, the other gray and purple. She'd ran out of blue yarn, she'd said and purple had been her favorite color back then. Elise had been thirteen. I'd just turned seventeen when she gave me these on Christmas Day. It had been a hard year. I'd moved out of my mom's house and into my dad's, hoping things at home would be better for me, only they hadn't. My dad had started a new family with a woman he barely knew and I was an afterthought.

"You made them for me. Of course I kept them."

She grins at me and tries them on, wiggling her fingers. "I'm glad I gave up knitting. These are awful."

While it was true that the weave wasn't tight enough to keep the cold out, they weren't awful. She'd spent hours working on them. Delicately crafting them with her own two hands. That meant something to me.

"I love you," I say, pulling each mitten off and setting them aside.

Elise falls back onto the pillows and tugs me

down on top of her. I love how confident she is, how she has no problem initiating physical intimacy between us.

She parts her legs and I nestle between them, softly rubbing my firm body over her soft one.

"Please don't hurt me," she whispers, breath trembling against my mouth.

I cradle her face in my hands and my heart aches when I meet her concerned gray eyes. "I hate that I hurt you before. I swear I was only trying to protect you."

"From what?" she murmurs.

"Me."

Elise brings her fingertips to my lips and touches them once before leaning in for a soft kiss. "You don't need to do that. I'm a big girl. I know what I want."

I shift beneath her, adjusting my inconvenient erection trapped between us. "Yeah? And what is it that you want?"

Without another word, she reaches one hand in between us, palming me through my pants, tempting me, wrapping me snugly in her fist. "This. You. Everything."

I sigh and find her mouth again, capturing it in a long kiss before finally pulling away. "You have me. My whole heart. I think you always did."

At my confession, she smiles and then the time for talking is done, because she works her hand under the elastic of my boxers and strokes me in long, lazy pulls that make me groan softly against her lips.

I've never been vocal during sex in my entire life. Never really released a grunt or a moan or anything. I was the strong silent type I guess you could say, but with Elise things are different. I can't keep my emotions in check when she's near, and evidently that extends to our lovemaking too. I praise her with gentle encouragement, groan when she orgasms around me, and communicate both with words and soft sighs to let her know when something feels good.

Thrusting into her fist, I tangle my hands in her hair and groan when she slides her hand down again. "You're too much. You know that?"

She shakes her head. "Never too much. Now kiss me."

And I do. A lot.

As easy as it is to lose myself in her, in this

moment, part of me is still aware that Owen could come home at any minute and the absolute last thing he'd want to hear were sex noises between me and his sister.

We've had enough close calls as it is.

I shift our positions on the bed so that I'm lying on my side facing her. Pulling her hand from my boxers, I kiss her wrist while she pretends to pout. At least I think she's pretending. "As much as I like that…I had something else in mind."

She grins, mouth pulling into a crooked smile as she looks at me. "You want to score."

"With you?" I lift my eyebrows. "Always."

Elise chuckles softly. "How can I say no to that?"

I lean close and press a chaste kiss to her lips. "Are you kidding? I have no idea how I got you to agree to date me in the first place. I feel like I won the fucking lottery."

Chuckling again, she wraps her arms around my neck, pulling me in for a slow, sweet kiss. But soon, my body has another idea and I'm eager for more, deepening our kiss and caressing every bare inch of her skin I can find.

"Baby," I whine, my dick already leaking pre-come in my boxers. "Get naked."

"Stop whining, big boy." She rises up on her knees with a teasing smirk and pulls her shirt off over her head.

I unclip her bra next and toss it over the side of the bed.

"That's better," I groan at the sight of her. Did I mention I've become more vocal in bed? I hardly recognize myself. Giving praise, raining down compliments, letting her know when something pleases me. It all comes so naturally now. It's almost freaking scary how right this feels, and part of me is worried I'm going to jinx it—jinx us if I focus on how perfect it is too much.

So instead I do what I do best, and focus on loving my girl. Which as it turns out, comes pretty naturally for me.

CHAPTER THIRTY-ONE

Naked Baby Photos

Justin

"Everything's just about ready," my mom calls from the kitchen. "You guys want to take your seats?"

I glance over at Elise who gives me the thumbs-up.

"Sure," I reply.

We're at my mom's house for Thanksgiving dinner, and later we'll go to Elise's parents' house for dessert, just like she suggested. I hadn't really wanted to come—I'm not all that close with my mother, but at Elise's encouragement, I'd reached out to my mom and she'd been so happy to have us over, and I guess I got caught up in the excitement. But it's actually going better than I thought it would.

I usher Elise to the dining table with my hand at the small of her back. After pulling out her chair and helping her settle in, I lean down and press a kiss to her lips. "You okay?"

She nods, looking chipper. "I'm doing great. I'm proud of you for coming."

I know what she means, that she's proud of me for manning up and setting aside my differences with my mom for the sake of the holiday. In a way, so am I. I haven't been home for a home cooked meal in what feels like years.

"And those baby pictures?" She lets out a soft chuckle. "Those were priceless."

I inwardly groan. Fifteen minutes into our visit my mom whipped out the baby albums, including the ones where I was naked in the bathtub as a toddler. *Fan-fucking-tastic*. Nothing undermines your masculinity like your girlfriend laughing at your childhood sized penis.

I narrow my eyes in mock disgust and shake my head. "I'll be right back."

Elise giggles again, trying to hold it together.

I head into the kitchen and watch my mom pour a sauce pan containing gravy into a small dish. Everything smells amazing.

"What can I help with?"

Mom shoves a platter of turkey at me. "I'm not one to refuse help in the kitchen. Carry this to the table?"

I nod. "Sure thing." I grab it along with a casserole dish filled with potatoes and make my way back to Elise. Mom joins us a second later with a dish of vegetables and dish filled with gravy in her hands. Elise pours the wine and then I say a small blessing and then we begin to eat.

It's been a long damn time since my mother cooked for me, and in some ways I'm still leery of being here, but in others, I'm glad Elise pushed me to do this. Plus, with her by my side, it makes everything easier. When I'd called my mom and told her I was dating Elise Parrish, she'd only laughed and said, 'about damn time.' I still chuckle that everyone had placed bets on us getting together when, all along, we were scared to take the plunge. Well, Elise wasn't. I was. The moment she whipped out the key to her apartment, I'd started sweating, filled with dread that I'd only end up hurting her. But Elise had called me on that too. I was scared. But I'm not anymore. I won't let my past dictate my future. I know what I want, and she's sitting right beside me.

I cut into my first bite of turkey and chew. "This is good, Mom."

She beams under my compliment, tears filling her eyes. "Thank you, son. I'm so happy you're home." She dabs her eyes with a cloth napkin. "Ugh. Look at me getting all emotional. I'm sorry."

I swallow and reach over to squeeze her shoulder.

"It's just…I'm so proud of you. Of the man you've become." She pauses, looking down at her barely touched plate. "Your father and I were young. We made a lot of mistakes."

I really don't feel like traipsing down memory lane. Especially not right now. All of this, my convoluted emotions, my messy family history, it won't be solved over one dinner, and frankly I'm not in the mood to get into this right now. Or ever.

"Mom," I say, my tone firm. "It's fine."

"I know it's hard to talk about, and we don't have to relive anything tonight. But I want you to know I love you, and I'm happy you're here." She puts her hand on mine. "And I want to make it up to you, so I hope you'll give me the chance."

"I love you too," I settle on. "Thanks for saying that."

Elise lifts her fork, taking a bite of her food, her eyes downcast.

After a few minutes of eating in awkward silence, I can't take it anymore. I launch into a story about the fight I got into during our last game, which has mom and Elise sharing conspiratorial looks.

"He used to be even worse," Mom says. "Always so aggressive on the ice."

Elise nods, not disagreeing.

Mom leans back, taking a sip of her wine as she appraises me, then Elise. "Honestly, I think I have you to thank, sweetie. My son has certainly calmed down. I'm not sure if you're aware—but he went through a bit of a slutty stage."

I blink in slo-mo. Did my mother just call me a slut?

Elise coughs into her napkin in an attempt to hide another laugh. "Um … You're welcome?"

They share a laugh—at my expense mind you—and then two sets of eyes swing my way.

Elise's gaze softens as she directs her attention back toward my mom. "Thank you for raising a good man with a good heart. Underneath all that slutty behavior, he really is a keeper," she adds.

I groan. "Come on, I'm right fucking here."

They laugh again. Elise reaches under the table to pat my leg, leaving her delicate palm on my knee. She can try to console me all she wants, but I'm pretty sure once we're alone later, I'm going to spank her sexy ass. It's that thought that makes me grin.

It's safe to say my mom and my girlfriend are going to get along great. And even though I'm not super close with my parents, it still feels good to have her acceptance. Elise is part of my future, and it feels amazing to have her by my side—yes, even when she and my mom are ganging up on me.

With Elise by my side, I'm learning I can pretty much tackle any obstacle head on. Which is good, because Owen and I still haven't had that talk he told me needed to happen. And I'm guessing we need to do that sooner rather than later before shit gets any weirder between us.

CHAPTER THIRTY-TWO

Happy Freaking Holidays

Elise

"So…. what's new?" Dad asks in a cheery tone from across the able, his gaze oscillating between my brother and my boyfriend.

My *boyfriend.* That still sounds so strange to me …. It's going to take some getting used to—in a good way.

Owen grunts and rolls his shoulders. We're all together—one big, *happy-ish* family—celebrating Thanksgiving at my parents' house. We'd had the main festivities with Justin's mom earlier today and now that the sun has set, we're just sitting down at the table for some pie with my parents and brother. We survived our first family outing earlier—and now I pray that we'll make it through this one too.

Dad's eyes swing over to Justin next and stay

there while he waits for a response that I'm pretty sure isn't coming. Ever since we arrived here fifteen minutes ago, I swear Owen hasn't said three words. And Justin has said exactly four. *Hello, everyone. Happy Thanksgiving.*

This is just so weird. I hate the thought that things have become strained between my brother and Justin, but I guess it's normal for there to be an adjustment period. Right? At least that's what I'm telling myself.

I poke at the slice of pumpkin pie on the plate in front of me with my fork and say a silent prayer for the floor to open up and swallow me whole. I'm pretty sure that'd be better than sitting through this awkward, uncomfortable silence.

"With the team, I mean," Dad clarifies at the silence still permeating my parent's formal dining room. "Anything new?"

I clear my throat and look to my mom, who looks almost just as panicked as I feel. I had given her a heads-up when we talked earlier this week that there might still be some lingering tension between Owen and Justin over our new relationship status, but I hoped it was nothing that couldn't be solved with dessert and alcohol. Emphasis on the *alcohol*. True to form, Mom had supplied everyone with a stiff beverage as soon as we'd come through the front door of my childhood home. Thank God for small blessings.

Dad's bushy gray eyebrows pinch together, and then he shakes his head once before forking a large bite of apple pie into his mouth.

"The pie is amazing, Mom," I say, slightly breathless. She smiles, but her lips are pulled into a firm line, and I realize with embarrassment that I haven't actually tasted the pie in front of me yet, so I rectify that, bringing a bite to my mouth and chewing slowly, like everything is totally normal.

"Look, can we just …" Justin starts, setting his fork down beside his plate and rubbing one hand over the back of his neck. There's a line creasing his forehead and he looks concerned. I have no idea what he's about to say. But one thing is certain, he couldn't take the silence anymore either. "Can we just clear the air a bit here? I'm dating Elise now. I know that might be weird for you guys, or that it might have come out of left field, or whatever, but I love her. I love your daughter, Mr. and Mrs. Parrish."

My mom smiles again and this time, it's genuine, her blue-ish gray eyes crinkling in the corners as she looks between us.

"And Owen, I…" Justin's speech is interrupted by my father raising his right hand—the one still holding the fork—and he's shaking his head.

"It's not weird at all, son. Elise's mom and I, we respect you. We watched you grow up, and we know you weren't necessarily dealt the best hand. You didn't have an easy time of it, and we know you've done extremely well for yourself. We're proud of you."

Tears threaten to fill my eyes, because I didn't know it, but this was exactly what I needed to hear. I needed my family's acceptance. But my dad's not done.

"And as long as Elise is happy," he adds, "we're happy. And we're more than supportive of a relationship between the two of you."

My mom reaches across the table and gives my dad's shoulder a squeeze. "What he said. We love you both."

Justin manages a thank you, and I barely hold my tears inside, blinking rapidly to clear my vision.

The dessert set before us has been forgotten, because now four sets of eyes swing over to Owen. His expression is stern, and he's staring down at the table in front of him.

God, why is he making this so awkward?

I'm not sure I could pinpoint what his issue is with me and Justin dating, even if you offered me a million dollars. Does he really think Justin's days of being a player (off the ice) aren't over? Does he think Justin will cheat on me? Break my heart? That we're not actually in love simply because Justin didn't have a good parental example of love growing up?

I've never seen Owen bothered by something quite so much. He's always been the easy-going, down for fun, playful type. But the tense energy flowing off him in waves is hard to ignore.

"Owen?" I ask, voice coming out soft. "Can you say something, please? Anything."

Finally, Owen clears his throat and looks up, locking eyes with Justin. "This is going to sound stupid."

My heart melts a little at the fact he's going to open up. I have no idea what's on his mind, but I'm thankful he's going to talk to us, finally. And it's only natural that he's got thoughts about this. I'm just dying to know what they are, what his objections could possibly be to me being happy and treated well in a committed relationship. Because seriously, bro …

He's still looking across the table at Justin, still baring that same weird expression—it's a mix between angry and hurt. "You've never been in a relationship before…"

I hold up my hand, ready to jump in and defend Justin, when he stops me by placing one hand gently against my spine.

"Let him finish," Justin says softly, leaning in toward me.

I take a deep breath and nod, gesturing for Owen to continue.

Owen sighs, leaning in to look at Justin. "You're my best friend. You've been by my side through team trades and draft picks, and injuries, and playoff games. We've shared an apartment for years now, and every hotel room while on the road for longer than that. Hell, you're the only person I could call that time I was tied up and…" He looks down at his lap and shakes his head, and Justin does the same.

Oh God, not the sex emergency.

Owen sighs and looks back up. "Anyway, you've always been the one I can count on, and I appreciate that."

Justin nods, acknowledging him at a brief pause in Owen's monologue. "Absolutely man, and it's been a crazy good ride. I wouldn't change that for anything."

Owen swallows. "But that's just it. Change is inevitable now. You're in a relationship with Elise, and I'm not so dense that I don't see that it's going to change us. Our friendship. Everything."

That's what he's worried about? For a second, I'm speechless. His little bro-mance with Justin? But then everything starts to click. With sadness, I finally get it. Owen's worried he's going to lose his best friend. His best friend of twenty-plus years. I'm about to open my mouth and tell him I would never let that happen, that I'd never stand in the way of their friendship, when it suddenly occurs to me, he's right. To a certain extent, their relationship has already begun to change—and I'm sure Owen feels that. Their days of prowling the bars hunting for girls are over. Their nights of double dates, and wild stories, and being each other's wingman are done. Part of me feels sad for Owen, but the rest of me is thinking *boo-fucking-hoo, dude*. Maybe it's time to grow the heck up. I clear my throat, and look to Justin before I say something that's probably going to come across as insensitive.

"I get it man, trust me, I do," Justin says, leaning forward to place his elbows on the table, looking directly at Owen. "And I know you think things are going to change now that I'm out of the game, so to speak, but you and I both know I haven't been … ah," he looks at me once, narrowing his eyes as if he's selecting his words carefully, "playing the game for a while now. Even before Elise, it had all grown stale to me."

Owen considers this, nodding once. "Yeah, I guess you're right."

"But I promise you," Justin adds. "You're my best friend. And I'll always make time for you. I've got your back. Just like I know you've got mine. And it means the world that you trust me with your sister. I promise I'm going to be good to her."

Owen raises his bottle of beer in a toast. "I know you will. And I'm glad you both understand that you're stuck with me."

Justin grins, and joins him, clinking his own beer against Owen's before taking a long drink. "We're not going anywhere," he reassures him.

I rise to my feet, and round the table to throw my arms around my brother's shoulders. "I love you, big bro."

"Yeah, yeah. Love you too," he grumbles, but he's smiling.

My dad clears his throat and all eyes in the room swing his way once again. "Relationship drama out of the way… is it safe to ask what's new with the team now?" Dad asks and we all begin laughing.

EPILOGUE

Elise

"**N**icely done," I greet Justin with a soft kiss pressed to his scruffy cheek. They won their game tonight against their long-time rivals from Denver, and so everyone is in the mood to celebrate. Which is why Becca, the girls and I came over to the bar we like near the rink to secure some tables. The guys have been filtering in over the last ten minutes as they finished up with showers and brief media interviews. All in a night's work, I guess.

Justin grins down at me, his hands sliding down to cup my behind. "Thank you."

I swat his hands away. "We're in public," I hiss.

He only chuckles. He does that a lot lately—laughs. I don't think I'll ever get tired of it. Our friends try to give me the credit for this change in him, they say he's not such a grumpy bastard any-more, and while they like to tease us, deep down, I know it's true. I make him happy. And I love that.

"Later then," he whispers, pressing a tender kiss to my temple.

I nod in agreement. We've had an active, and exceptional, sex life. I never knew sex could be so much fun, but it is. There's nothing to be self-conscious about, no awkward moments whatsoever. There's just me, and the man I love and a whole lot of chemistry.

We settle in together on one side of a booth, and the waitress comes by to take Justin's order as he loosens his tie. I already have a cocktail in front of me.

Owen and Teddy are in the corner arguing over the best whiskeys, and other idiotic shit like who would win in a fight—a grizzly bear or a shark. I can't even with those two. It's like puberty skipped over them—leaving them in man-sized bodies with the emotional maturity of fourteen-year-olds.

Becca looks a little somber tonight. I've promised her that nothing about our friendship will change just because I'm in a relationship. The look she gave me said she wants to believe me, but she's not so sure. She's nursing a margarita at the far end of the table, listening to whatever Sara's whispering to her, but her eyes are on my brother. I don't think Owen even notices her. As close as they are, he can be a little clueless sometimes.

But before I can ponder it further, Justin leans close, pushing my hair over my shoulder so he can plant a soft, damp kiss to the side of my neck that makes my toes curl.

"I love you, Elise." His voice is deep and raspy, and my eyes swing over to his.

"I love you too." I touch his jaw, wondering about the sudden emotion I feel flowing between us.

A second later I see movement from the corner of my vision. "Enough you two. Just because you're dating my sister now doesn't mean I can't still kick your ass, Brady."

It's my brother. He places one hand on Justin's shoulder and gives it a firm squeeze, but his expression is playful.

"Good game tonight," I say, grinning up at Owen. For all his faults, my brother is a damn good hockey player.

"Thanks." He takes a long drink of his beer, his eyes roaming over toward a group of single ladies seated at the bar. I saw them when I came in—I think it's a bachelorette party. I was hoping Owen wouldn't notice them. No such luck.

"Hey." I tug his shirt sleeve, getting his attention. Owen gazes down at me. "Will you go check on Becca?"

"Becca?" He frowns, his eyes swinging over to where she sits, contemplatively gazing down into an empty margarita glass. "I'm sure she's fine," he says, his tone non-committal.

"Owen," I say firmly, my tone a warning.

He shrugs, relenting. "I'll check on her. As soon as I assess the situation at the bar. Bridal parties are my jam." Turning toward where Teddy sits, he makes a lewd hand gesture, then motions toward the bar. "Let's roll, baby."

Teddy chuckles, and gets up to follow him. *God, they are idiots.*

I take a deep breath, trying to calm myself so I don't have to castrate my brother or his friends when I feel Justin's calming hand press between my shoulder blades, rubbing gently. It calms me almost instantly. "You okay, babe?" His chiseled features are drawn into a tight line, and his expression is unreadable.

I smile, trying to reassure him. "Fine. I'm sure everything's fine. It's just sometimes my brother is such a jackass."

"There's no denying that." He leans closer, nuzzling his face into my neck. "I have to agree with you on that...but I may think he's an idiot for different reasons than you. If it's any consolation, though, I love you."

"I know you do. And can I just say I'm so glad your manwhore days are behind you?"

He chuckles then, his lips grazing my jawline again. "I am too, sweetheart. I am too." He kisses me once softly on the lips and then meets my eyes. "I've got everything I need right here."

It might sound cheesy, but he's right. We have each other, and it feels like everything I could ever want or need with this gorgeous, thoughtful man. I guess the rest of the guys will just have to figure that out on their own. I only hope it's sooner rather than later for Owen's sake.

• • •

I hope you enjoyed Justin and Elise's story … up next is Becca and Owen and I can't wait to share what happens next! Let's just say the story starts with a BANG! If you're ready for more hot hockey players, check out **ALL THE WAY**, details on the next page.

ALL THE WAY

CHAPTER ONE

Drunken Confessions

Owen

"**C**ome on, that's it. Nice and easy. One step at a time."

With my hands on her hips, I guide Becca slowly down the hallway toward my bedroom and away from our friends still partying hard, including my sister, Elise, and my best friend, Justin, who have recently become an item.

"But I'm not even tired," Becca says, a huge yawn interrupting her in the middle of that statement. "I could keep going for hours."

I chuckle. "Right. Humor me, then."

Our group of friends had gone out for some drinks to celebrate after we obliterated our opponents in tonight's hockey game, and then several of us ended up back here at my place to continue the celebration.

It's almost two in the morning, and like any good friend would do, I'm helping a very drunk Becca to my room where she can sleep it off, since there's no way I'm putting her in an Uber with a stranger, not in this state or at this time of night. That's definitely not happening.

"Take my bed. I can sleep on the couch in the media room," I say after steering her into my room.

I close the door behind us, shutting out the noise of the party. Most people have gone home by now, but there are still a couple of guys hanging out in the living room.

"You mean you're actually going to take a break from sleeping around tonight?" she murmurs, her voice playful and a little surprised.

"I don't sleep around that much."

Okay, yeah, I do, but still, I don't know why she's calling me on it. Becca and I have been friends for years, and she's never commented on my overly enthusiastic sex life. Just like I don't comment on hers, or the lack of it. Which is exactly the way I prefer it. I've never let myself think about Becca as anything but a friend.

While she sits on the edge of my bed to remove her boots and socks, I hunt around in my dresser for a clean T-shirt she can wear to sleep in. When I turn to hand it to her, she's halfway through undressing, her pants unbuttoned as she tries to shove them down her hips, awkwardly and with a lot of grunting.

I toss the T-shirt on the bed beside her and turn my back to give her some privacy.

She seems unconcerned right now about putting on a free show, but I know in the morning she'll be horrified to learn she did that. Becca is normally so modest and composed. I don't remember the last time I saw her get drunk like this.

"I'm safe now. You can look."

When I turn, she's standing across from me dressed in a soft gray T-shirt with my team's logo that engulfs her five-foot-four frame, hitting her below the knees. She looks so small, I can't help but grin at her.

"You good now?"

"Yup. But don't lie to me, Owen." She takes a step closer and jabs her finger at my chest. "I know you better than you think."

I smirk at her. "Oh yeah? And what is it that you think you know?"

I'm suddenly a little worried about what she might say next.

My sexual appetite isn't exactly a secret. Ever since making it to the pros, I've indulged probably a little more than was necessary, but I have no qualms about this. I'm young and single, living my best life after years of hard work and dedication to my sport.

I'm having fun, and no one gets hurt by false promises of more than one night. And I'm sure as hell not ready to settle down. But now with Becca looking at me like I'm a puzzle she wants to solve, I find myself feeling a little uneasy.

She purses her lips, thinking. "Honestly? I kind of wish I could be like you."

She wishes she could sleep around? That's news to me. Not to mention, any guy in his right mind would be perfectly happy to introduce her to the business end of his dick.

I'm transported back to our chat last week when we met for coffee. Listening to Becca complain about her dating life, I thought it was nothing more than a little dry spell, but now I'm starting to think maybe there's a lot more to it than that.

"Um, why?" I manage next.

"I wish I could have a more relaxed attitude like you have about sex. You just seem to enjoy yourself and have a good time and not overthink it, I guess. That's all."

I shift my weight, realizing how close we're standing. "Yeah, that's true. I enjoy it for what it is."

Something doesn't add up. Becca is a good girl. She's not the kind of girl who does casual hook-ups—she's the kind of girl you settle down with once you've sowed your wild oats and are ready for monogamy.

She reaches up, patting my chest, whispering and giggling at the same time. "You know, there are rumors that you have a really big dick. I've been on message boards and seen girls talk about him—I mean it."

I almost swallow my tongue. Drunk Becca is freaking hilarious and has absolutely no filter. What exactly does one say to that? "Thank you" feels inappropriate. And I'm certainly not going to disagree with her, so I opt to stay quiet.

"Okay, then." I clap my hands together once. "Enough with the bedtime stories. It's time for you to sleep off the booze."

She drops onto my bed, sighing dramatically, and as she does, the T-shirt I gave her rides up her thighs, giving me a clear view of her panties beneath.

They're light blue. Cotton. Basic. And still sexy as hell.

I swallow and take a deep breath. "Becca, close your legs."

She sits cross-legged and looks up at me. "Hmm?"

"I can see your panties." I make a point of looking down at her lap and swallow. "Please close your legs."

She seems unconcerned about this, probably because she's so comfortable with me. And it's not like they're even sexy panties, but my body doesn't care.

Becca is gorgeous, poised, sweet, and smart. Just because we've always stayed firmly in the friend zone doesn't mean I don't notice how attractive she is. You'd have to be blind not to.

I should tuck her in and leave. I definitely shouldn't be standing here ogling her like she's on tonight's menu. She's a good friend to my younger sister, Elise, and she's a good friend to me, one of the only females I'm close friends with. She works at the arena, and I cannot, will not fuck anything up by objectifying her.

"You'll be comfortable in here, right?" I hear myself asking.

She nods and smiles. "Thank you, Owen. What would I do without you?"

I suck in a harsh breath between my teeth. "Becca. Your legs."

"I mean, here I am all broken, and you're being so sweet to me."

"You're not broken." My voice has a hard edge to it, and I clear my throat, trying again in a softer tone. "Why would you say that?"

I know her history, and it's awful. It makes my blood boil just thinking about it.

Becca survived a brutal attack her freshman year at college, and the upperclassman who tried to rape her only got a slap on the wrist. It was some bullshit technicality that the judge latched onto.

The deed hadn't been completed before the fuck-face was pulled off of Becca by a bystander, who I wish I could thank. Still, the attack left a lasting impression on Becca. I didn't know her then, but I do know she's been through years of counseling to deal with it, and still carries the emotional scars. How could you not?

She grabs my pillow and hugs it to her chest. "It's just, I want to move on, you know? I don't want to be defined by my past. But every time I get close to someone . . ."

"What?" I ask, stepping closer to the bed.

She shakes her head. "I don't know. I guess I'm just a big pussy when it comes to hooking up."

Realization of her choice of words hits her, and Becca starts laughing. "Pussy. Oh my God!" She clamps one hand over her mouth, still giggling.

I chuckle along with her. "You don't have to hook up and sleep around if you don't want to. There's nothing wrong with being choosy. Hell, I think it's a damn good thing."

She licks her lips, curling her legs under her in the center of my bed. "I know. It's just, I feel like I'm finally at a place where I want more, and I have no idea how to go and get it."

I'd already met her through Elise, but it was when Becca started working in the office at the arena that we became instant friends. I used to tease her about why she never dated, and then she finally told me the truth. She's dated casually but has a hard time trusting people and opening up, and anytime a man attempts to take it to the next level, she completely freezes up. Which makes sense, obviously.

"I mean, seriously, do you know how long it's been since I've been kissed?" Her eyes are wide and eager.

"I—don't."

"A long freaking time."

"Any man alive would be happy to kiss you." My voice comes out a little tight.

She nods. "It's what comes after the kissing that makes me nervous." Then she looks up and meets my eyes, her bright blue gaze inquisitive and demanding. "The only guy I'm comfortable with is you. I mean, if you wanted to take a break from all the bunnies and help me get back in the saddle . . ."

She starts giggling again, and my heart fucking stops.

"Saddle. Get it?" She chuckles, raising her eyebrows dramatically while she pokes me in the ribs.

I hope like fuck I'm hearing things, because otherwise I'm pretty sure Becca just suggested we have sex, and there's nothing about that scenario that makes any sense.

"How much have you had to drink tonight?" I ask, my voice sounding as tense as my body feels.

She taps her fingers to her chin, pondering this. "Two margaritas at the bar." She counts those on her slender fingers. Her nails are painted pale pink. "And then I think a couple of tequila shots when we got back here."

"Who let you have that much tequila?"

She shakes her head. "I'm fine. I'm not even that 'toxicated. Plus, this is the most genius plan I've ever had, really, Owen. It's brilliant."

Averting my eyes, I groan. "Please, for the love of God, close your legs."

"Huh. Why?"

"Because I can see your panties." For the fourth time.

"Oh, sorry."

Does she seriously think I'm mad? I'm about to go certifiably insane.

Becca twists one long dark lock of hair around her finger as her gaze wanders over my body. "I hope you haven't shaved your chest, because I love the hair on it."

I've never heard words like this come out of her mouth in the four years we've been friends. My heart begins to hammer against my ribs.

"I mean, I know you're probably a lot bigger than the toy I use, but we could at least try."

Toy? My mouth has gone bone dry. Focus, Owen.

"Becca, I'm not going to fuck you."

"Why not?"

Why not? Sweet fuck. I can't with her right now.

"Because. You have issues with intimacy and trust and . . ." My mind goes completely blank. Where the fuck am I going with this?

She's nodding. "Exactly. And you could help me get past those insecurities because I trust you completely, and we're besties."

I shake my head. "You should sleep it off."

Several tense seconds tick by. Neither of us moves.

"Can I just at least look at it?" Her words come barreling out, her tone hinting at annoyance.

She's annoyed with me? Oh, that's rich. I'm trying to do the right thing, and she's making my job ten times harder. Literally.

"Look at what?"

Her gaze drops to my crotch. "Your penis."

My eyebrows shoot up. "You want to look at my dick?"

"No. Well, yes. I mean, please, Owen. I need to prove to myself that there's nothing scary about this, right?"

Something painful squeezes inside my chest. She needs help remembering that men aren't scary, and she feels safe enough with me to not only talk about it, but also ask for my help.

Fuck. I rake my hands through my hair as my mind runs at a million miles an hour.

I would do anything for this girl. The moment I really got to know her, I became protective of her.

Even though her request is crazy, there's this achy feeling in the center of my chest for her.

"It's just a plain ol' wiener, right? Nothing to be scared of. But every time I even think about it . . ." She squeezes her eyes closed and gives her head a firm shake. "I freeze."

"Becca." I stop beside the bed and place one hand on her shoulder. Her eyes open and latch onto mine. "You can't be serious here."

"Just one quick peek before I go to sleep?" she asks again, those big blue eyes still peering hopefully up at mine.

Christ. Why won't she just drop this? Doesn't she know my self-control is hanging by a thread? I'm a guy . . . and a woman wants to see my junk, so, of course I'm actually contemplating it.

"I don't think that's a good idea." Understatement of the century.

She scoffs. "The guys in the locker room have probably seen it eight thousand times. It's not a big deal." She pouts, pushing out her lower lip.

Apparently, because I'm a masochist who has no problem showing off his dick, I start to soften to the idea. "One quick look, and then I'm leaving and you're going to sleep."

She bounces up and down on her knees, practically giddy. "Yes. I promise."

This is so fucking weird. Like a twisted version of show and tell.

"You've got ten seconds, Becca."

She nods in agreement.

I'm wearing athletic shorts, so it'll be simple to pull them down my hips. Yet there's nothing simple about the way Becca's gaze appraises me. Her brow is crinkled in concentration and her expression is serious. It's like she's studying for a damn calculus exam.

Sliding my hands under the waistband, I draw my shorts down a couple of inches and stop. The top of my manscaped pubic hair is visible now, but nothing else.

I watch Becca carefully, waiting for any signs that she's uncomfortable, that this is a horrible idea and I should slam on the brakes. But she bites her lip, her eyes wide as though she's waiting to unwrap a long-awaited Christmas present.

Fuck it. I'm already going to hell anyway, so I might as well fast-track this ride. I shove the shorts the rest of the way down until gravity does the rest and they drop to my ankles.

Thank fucking God I'm soft.

It's not a wish I've ever made in the presence of a beautiful woman before, but right now, I'm extremely thankful that my cock is, well, mostly soft. Our conversation over the past few minutes excited me for reasons unknown, but I managed to contain myself, for the most part. My dick hangs heavily beside my thigh, only slightly swollen in interest.

Becca leans closer. "Oh. That's . . ." She swallows, her gaze still glued to my crotch, and I'd give anything to know what she's thinking. "That's interesting," she finally says.

Interesting? My eyebrows shoot up. Not exactly what I wanted to hear. "Interesting?" I echo.

She nods, leaning closer. "It's just not what I was expecting."

I can't ask her what she was expecting, because the words lodge in my throat as she moves closer to the edge of the bed where I'm standing.

"May I?"

When she reaches toward me, I freeze. She isn't serious, is she?

"I can't see the whole thing."

Confused, I glance at myself to see it's lying down, covering my balls. I have no fucking idea what she intends to do, but I find myself nodding.

What.

The.

Actual.

Fuck.

Owen.

Carefully, like she's cradling a newborn puppy and not a dick—the dick attached to one of her best friends, mind you—Becca lifts it in her hand.

The second I feel her warm palm against me, I start hardening, and there's not a damn thing I can do about it. She's touching me, and my body doesn't seem to know the difference. It's game fucking on.

I count backward from a hundred and pinch the bridge of my nose with two fingers, inhaling a huge shuddering breath. "Hurry up. Your ten seconds are almost done," I hiss out.

The warmth of her delicate hand is shattering my self-control. I know this should feel weird and wrong, but it doesn't. Not at all. I hate that it doesn't. I need to put a stop to this, but apparently I suck at saying no to her.

I dare a glance down at Becca, and she's looking at me in wonder. "Oh, it's, um . . ." She lets out a nervous chuckle, her hand still gingerly wrapped around me. "It's getting harder."

I release a slow exhale, pressing the heel of my palm to my forehead. "Yeah, there's a woman touching it, in case you didn't notice."

"Oh, right." She drops me immediately and holds up both hands, her palms facing me. "Sorry. I'm done now."

I tug up my shorts and tuck my now fully erect dick behind the waistband. Just fucking fantastic.

I pull back the sheet on my bed and gesture for her to climb in. When she does, I pull the blankets up over her, tucking her in securely like my mom used to do to me when I was little.

"Get some sleep." I turn off the lamp beside my bed, leaving only a small sliver of light peeking in under the door from the hallway.

As I make my way to the door, she yawns and then whispers, "Thanks, Owen. You're the best.

That didn't even freak me out, so I think you definitely helped me."

My heart squeezes again, and I nod in her direction. "Good night, angel."

Outside in the hall, I close the door to my bedroom and lean up against it. My head falls back with a thud, and I close my eyes.

Fucking hell.

I can't believe that just happened. I can't believe I let that happen. I can't believe how fucking good her hand felt. Fuck.

Voices come from Justin's bedroom, and I realize that he and Elise are talking. The door is open, so I stop as I walk past, leaning against the door frame to peer in at them.

"Hey," I say softly.

Elise looks at me and apparently reads something in my expression. "What's wrong? Is Becca okay?"

Define okay? I rake one hand through my hair and blow out a sigh. "Can I talk to you?"

"Sure," my younger sister says, her voice a little uneasy like she already knows something's wrong.

She's too damn perceptive for her own good.

She follows me out into the hall but I keep going, heading toward the media room, which thankfully is now empty. I doubt Becca would want anyone to overhear this conversation, and I intend to make sure we have privacy. We enter, and I take a seat on the couch while Elise remains standing.

I search for the right words to say as she looks down at me expectantly.

So, Becca just touched my dick . . .

Yeah, that's not going to work.

"What happened? You're freaking me out," Elise snaps.

Stalling, I lick my lips, still in complete shock about what just happened in my room. God, I can still feel the warmth of Becca's hand if I close my eyes.

"If you touched her, Owen, so help me God . . ." Elise plants one hand firmly on her hip.

"I didn't touch her," I croak out, shaking my head.

"Then what happened?"

"She wanted to . . ." I swallow. Nope. Can't say

that either. "She touched me—but just for a second." Well, ten to be exact.

Elise lets out a noise of angry surprise. "What the hell? Why would you let her do that?"

"I know. Fuck. I shouldn't have. But she said something about not wanting to be afraid anymore, and that she trusts me."

Elise frowns and then sighs. "Oh, Becca."

"It'll be okay. Hopefully, she won't remember any of this tomorrow."

At least, that's what I'm banking on.

• • •

Get Your Copy of All the Way

www.kendallryanbooks.com/books/all-the-way

Special Bonus Scene

Wonder what happened when Justin & Elise rescued Owen from his sex emergency?

Read on for a special bonus scene ....

Justin

As I enter the bedroom, two things happen simultaneously. The first is that my eyes are assaulted by the vision of my best friend naked. *Gah! The second is that my stomach tightens as I take in the scene around him.*

He's bent over at the waist and handcuffed to the headboard. Lying on the floor between his parted feet is a purple glittery dildo.

What the actual fuck?

Owen groans in relief when he sees me. "Thank God. Took you long enough. Get me the fuck out of here."

The uneasy feeling inside my chest grows with each step closer I take. "What the fuck happened, dude?"

Owens hesitates for a second, hanging his head. "Revenge happened."

My eyebrows jump up. "This was a revenge fuck?"

Owen doesn't answer right away, he just hangs his head in shame.

I locate the key to the handcuffs on a nearby dresser and get to work unlocking each of his wrists while trying not to make eye contact with any exposed body parts. I've seen it all before in the locker room, but this just feels different. It feels fucking wrong.

He grunts as finally free him, rubbing at his wrists which each bear a faint red mark.

"I guess that wasn't the first time I picked up that redhead from the bar. And when she realized I didn't remember her, she freaked out. In my defense, it was two years ago, and she'd cut her hair."

"So she just left you like this?" I look up at the ceiling while he locates his boxers and jeans and begins getting dressed.

"It was a little more involved than that," Owen says, his eyes wandering to his purple glittery friend on the floor.

For a second I consider ignoring the elephant in the room, because part of me really does *not* want to know the particulars of this little sexcapade gone wrong. But then the logical part of my brain points out that this situation Owen's found himself in could provide ammunition for years to come. And knowing I'll be able to hang this over his head anytime I want something? Well, let's just say I'm willing to put my own discomfort aside in favor of knowing the truth.

"So did she...?"

"Yup."

"And the ..." My eyes stray toward the toy left behind.

"You don't want to know," he snaps.

"Oh but I do." I grin wryly.

Owen groans and shakes his head, as if dislodging a painful memory. "Can we please just fucking go?"

I hold up one hand. "Fine. You're right. I probably don't want to know."

"Damn right you don't. And I can't believe you

brought my sister."

I shrug. "She was worried. We were all out together when I got your text."

He exhales slowly, grabbing his discarded shirt from the floor. "Let's go."

"Happily. After you," I remark.

Owen stops me at the door to the hallway with a hand pressed into my chest. "And if you tell any of the guys about this, I will fucking end you."

I grin. "How about *thank you, Justin for saving my ass*. Literally," I add.

He rolls his eyes and heads out the door to face Elise.

Acknowledgements

I would like to thank Elaine York and Rachel Brookes for the guidance on this book, and Dana Sulonen, a sports editor in Detroit who covers hockey, for making sure I didn't take too many liberties while fictionalizing my hockey romance. Rose Hilliard at Audible you are a gem, and I was delighted to work with you on this project. Virginia Tesi-Carey, you are a proofreading goddess! A huge thank you to Sarina Bowen for your sage advice on this story.

Thank you so much to my incredible readers. I hope you enjoyed this story. I had a blast writing about this fictional hockey team, and I'm looking forward to getting to know each and every player a little bit more as I continue the series.

And remember, every reader deserves a hot hero and a happy ending!

Get Two Free Books

Sign up for my newsletter and I'll automatically send you two free books.

www.kendallryanbooks.com/newsletter

Follow Kendall

BookBub has a feature where you can follow me and get an alert when I release a book or put a title on sale. Sign up here to stay in the loop:

www.bookbub.com/authors/kendall-ryan

Website

www.kendallryanbooks.com

Facebook

www.facebook.com/kendallryanbooks

Twitter

www.twitter.com/kendallryan1

Instagram

www.instagram.com/kendallryan1

Newsletter

www.kendallryanbooks.com/newsletter

About the Author

A *New York Times*, *Wall Street Journal*, and *USA TODAY* bestselling author of more than two dozen titles, Kendall Ryan has sold over two million books, and her books have been translated into several languages in countries around the world. Her books have also appeared on the *New York Times* and *USA TODAY* bestseller list more than three dozen times. Kendall has been featured in publications such as *USA TODAY*, *Newsweek*, and *In Touch Magazine*. She lives in Texas with her husband and two sons.

To be notified of new releases or sales, join Kendall's private Mailing List.

www.kendallryanbooks.com/newsletter

Get even more of the inside scoop when you join Kendall's private Facebook group, Kendall's Kinky Cuties:

www.facebook.com/groups/kendallskinkycuties

Other Books by Kendall Ryan

Unravel Me
Filthy Beautiful Lies Series
The Room Mate
The Play Mate
The House Mate
The Impact of You
Screwed
The Fix Up
Dirty Little Secret
xo, Zach
Baby Daddy
Tempting Little Tease
Bro Code
Love Machine
Flirting with Forever
Dear Jane
Finding Alexei
Boyfriend for Hire
The Two Week Arrangement
Seven Nights of Sin

For a complete list of Kendall's books, visit:

www.kendallryanbooks.com/all-books/

Made in the USA
Coppell, TX
17 April 2020